Orgasmo

Donald O'Donovan

Published by Open Books

Cover image Copyright © by Mark K. Hollinger MKH

Learn more about the artist at
https://www.facebook.com/pages/Mark-K-Hollinger-Photography/235692010046

ISBN: 0615904599

ISBN-13: 978-0615904597

1

*I*ce cream melts, youth ends, beauty fades, love dies. A whole century, gone like a glass of water. And now I'm alone.

This crumbling old hotel on Sonrisa Street is a Dante's Inferno inhabited by the misbegotten, the unfit, the unsalvageable. The tenants are dipsomaniacs, somnambulists, criminal psychopaths, pathetic retirees and Mexican junkies. In the room next to mine lives a phony Gypsy lady who tells fortunes and turns tricks, and next door to her a pair of blond morphodites, retired circus freaks, both of them midgets. Down the hall in this chamber of horrors you'll find a stuttering waiter who munches a dry herring wrapped in a Yiddish newspaper, Mr. Plaah or Mr. Plaargh, and he's wanted for armed robbery.

I said I was alone, but I have a miserable little drowned rat of a dog here with me. I don't know where she came from. She's no more company than a cockroach, but at least she doesn't eat much. We went for a walk this morning on Hollywood Boulevard and a man said to me, "I'll give you a dollar for that dog." I almost took it.

"The first thing an artist should learn is how to use a gun." A phrase of Byron's. I've written it in huge looping letters on my wall with a red crayon.

Byron Lovelace insists that Sol Fingerbein is *a frotteur*—that is, he gets his kicks by rubbing women's behinds on the RTD. Sol has only to brush a firm ass with the back of his hand, so Byron says, and he spasms, like a purple sea squirt. "His expression," Byron confides, "is what kills me." His face goes rigid—beads of sweat pop out on his forehead—his mustache zigs and zags. "Then a spot of moisture appears on his pants, near the fly."

I can't vouch for the truth of this story of Byron's. As a matter of fact, when Byron told it to me, about a year ago in his studio, I somehow had the impression that he was talking about himself.

Fausto claims that he's lost his destiny. "Not only my destiny, but my soul, my friend. I feel like a snake that has shed its skin—except that I'm the skin and not the snake." He told me this yesterday morning at Clifton's Cafeteria.

Fausto's not the only one who's lost his soul. I've got the same problem. Thanks to Marlena. It was the book that did it. Her autobiography. I wrote Marlena's autobiography, and that was my undoing. For Marlena read Alma Delia Mortadella and for Alma Delia Mortadella read Lilith and for Lilith read Kali the Destroyer. I wrote her story, not mine. And that was a mistake. I became her—flesh of my flesh. Marlena was my world and the womb in which I gestated, a rutabaga with tube feet, a cauliflower drunk with words.

A dream, last night, a dream about Marlena, a dream blackened around the edges by the blackness of my despair. We were making love on her big fluffy pink bed in the middle of Hollywood Boulevard. The bed was mounted on casters and her husband—the half-man—had attached his motorized wheelchair to the headboard and he was towing us down Hollywood Boulevard as if we were a float in the Easter Parade.

"I'm fucking your wife, you crippled bastard!" I shouted. "I'm fouling the nest! I'm soaking her bush with my gysm! She's mine, I tell you. She's mine!"

We're approaching Hollywood and Las Palmas, the enormous flamingo-pink Angelyne billboard. Our bed is flirting with traffic. I'm gazing deep into Marlena's eyes, licking her tongue, frantically biting her hair. I can feel the orgasms welling up behind her ovaries like a legion of blind seagulls.

I got a call from Starz, Milton LaStarza, a cinematographer on the skids. Or at least that's how I remembered him. We'd both been poor in Paris, but life's a grand adventure when you're young, and we never minded being without things like toilet paper, deodorant and toothpaste. Later on, of course, there's no denying that lengthy binges landed Starz more than once in the street. But now, apparently, the lad's desperado days were behind him.

"I'm back, man," he told me on the phone. "I'm really back. I had lunch yesterday with Danny DeVito and Naomi Watts."

Starz was on a roll. A beach house in Malibu and let's work together on a script. I was impressed, and it really was good to hear from Starz again. I didn't have two nickels but I grabbed a taxi to Malibu and sure enough, Starz emerged from the beach house and paid with a couple of crisp Benjamins. A smashing escort service girl was just leaving. She took my taxi, in fact.

We went inside, sat on a landing barge-sized divan overlooking the Pacific Ocean and passed the bong, and Starz poured us each a Cutty and water. Starz looked good, I have to say that. His hair was short and spiky and he'd grown a prickly blond beard. Starz was in fact a regular prickly pear of a man, always getting into situations. Wherever he landed he'd stick like a burr, and soon there'd be a ruckus of some sort. Starz had big dreams, grandiose dreams if you like, but he had the stuff to make them come true, too—or at least I thought he did. He'd been a Steadicam operator in Hollywood before he started in on the sauce. I was feeling pretty optimistic.

"You remember Chief Dan George?" Starz began as we clinked our glasses, "Great guy, a natural actor. Remember in *Little Big Man* when the Chief said that thing about a pleasant show of enthusiasm? That's what I told Bambi, that girl who just left. You saw her, didn't you? What did you think? No, wait—before you answer, listen to this. *What do you expect for three hundred bucks?* That's what she said to me. *What do you expect for three hundred bucks?* 'What do I expect for three hundred bucks?' I said. 'I'll tell you what I expect for three hundred bucks. A pleasant show of enthusiasm! That's what I expect for three hundred bucks. A pleasant show of enthusiasm!' "

We went back outside and inspected his six-foot San Pedro cactus, and then he told me about Sylvia.

"This, all of this, the beach house, the pool, the BMW, is Sylvia's. None of this is mine, you understand. I just happened along, like Br'er Rabbit. I hopped into her life."

"She adopted you?"

"Something like that. We met on the Internet. She's divorced. She's a landscape painter, beautiful stuff. I'll show you tomorrow." He glanced at his watch. "Say, do you want to get some girls?"

"Maybe later. Let's talk about the script."

"Script? There's no script. It's all in *here*. A beautiful reporter is possessed by the soul of a girl who was murdered by her evil stepfather twenty years before. She hires a handsome exorcist who promptly gets possessed by the ghost of the stepfather. So they're going to play it all over again, the murder, a rerun. Unless..."

"Unless what?"

"You tell me. How does she get away from this guy?"

"Let's see... She meets another handsome guy, an archer, in the woods."

"Okay, good."

"He's carrying a compound bow."

"I like it."

"Then they meet a hermit who tells them that if they dip an arrow in the reporter's blood and shoot it into the exorcist's heart the stepfather's ghost will split and the curse will be lifted."

"Does the exorcist die?"

"No."

"Somebody's gotta die. This is a fucking horror film, man."

"Well, the stepfather dies. That's the idea."

"More. We need blood. The exorcist dies. Tell me the exorcist dies."

"Okay, he dies. The exorcist dies and the stepfather dies."

"What about the hermit? Does he die?"

"Okay, he dies. The hermit dies..."

The next day we went sailing. "Any dumbfuck can drive a powerboat," Starz told me, "but sailing is an art and a science. The beauty of the sunfish is that you can sail at a tight angle upwind." I was scared but I didn't let on. It was beautiful, I have to admit. We were racing across the water, completely silent except for the waves crashing on our bow and the howling wind.

That night we went to dinner at the Seven Seas, a posh restaurant owned by Sylvia's ex, Norm. We both ordered the king crab. Norm came to our table and shook hands. He was Italian, big, sinister. But Norm was a prince, it turned out. When it came time to pay we found out he'd comped us, king crab, champagne, the works. After dinner we went to the Las Palmas Dance Hall downtown, a taxi-dance joint across the street from the old United Artists Building. It's a great place for buying affection if you've got the jack. I danced with Svetlana. She was Russian. Svetlana wanted a hundred bucks to go to a hotel. I didn't have that kind of money on me and it was too early in the game to be hitting Starz up for a loan.

A week went by, then two. We'd become regulars at Las Palmas, and our days were filled with eating and drinking. Starz would order out—pizza, Chinese, crab cakes Dijon and veal scaloppini from Café Spruzzo, or filet mignon, lobster, you name it. Nothing was too good for us.

"My God, it's been so long since I felt like a human being," I almost said one fine sunny afternoon as we were sitting in the gazebo with a bottle of Bollinger and spoonfuls of beluga on little crackers, but I caught myself in time. You should never let people—even close friends—know how desperate you are. It scares them off.

The script was moving right along. We'd talk, then I'd go and type. I started running lines with Svetlana. She was an aspiring actress, it turned out, like all the girls at Las Palmas, like all of the girls at all of the dime-a-dance joints in LA, dreaming their Hollywood dreams while they dance with lonely desperate men who are dreaming about getting it on with them.

There was another issue. It had to do with Starz's mental state. Back before the Paris days Starz's moms had committed him to a lunatic asylum for 72 hours and he was afraid she was going to do it again, even though she was in Brooklyn and he was in California. As a result he was half nuts with paranoia. One day—so he said—he was tending to the sailboat and six squads of F-16s came screeching overhead at just a couple hundred feet. Starz dove for cover and banged his head on the dock. The next day he was out by the sailboat again and an Apache helicopter landed on the front lawn. That chopper was real. I saw it touch down just a few yards from the beach house, and a soldier in tan cammies got out packing an M-16. It was probably just maneuvers or something, but Starz was spooked and I had to admit it was pretty eerie.

Right after that Sylvia, Starz's quality woman, popped in, wearing a floppy hat. It's a type, these rich women with their floppy hats. They take you over. But Starz must have known what he was getting into when he put himself up for adoption. It was a pretty sweet deal, though. He didn't have to give her the time all that often, plus she was a nice looking woman for sixty-one. I saw right away however that Sylvia disapproved of me. I guess she could tell I wasn't a member of the cucumber sandwich set.

Then Starz latched onto Svetlana. I should have seen it coming when they started in on the Banana Kush and the vodka. It was a thing with them, right from the get-go, as though they'd invented that particular combination. Svetlana was crazy about the sailing, too, another item they had in common. And then they ganged up on me about the blood. "We need more blood." They were united on that. So I wrote in a flashback of the original murder. "The stepfather stabs her eighty-one times with a flensing knife," I told them. "Then a woodsman chops the stepfather's head off with a double-bitted ax." I made Svetlana run the lines with me. She knew I was pissed off, and she understood perfectly well that I was the woodsman and that it was Starz's head I wanted to chop off, not the stepfather's.

This calamity didn't sink our boat, but the next one did. Sylvia threw a huge party at the beach house, entertaining a regular battalion of her upscale New York friends, a local poetry circle and a glittery Polish count who swept her off her feet that very night. This new twosome, Sylvia and the Count, were resonant of the handsome archer and the beautiful reporter in my screenplay, so I wrote them into the script, as doppelgangers to my regular characters. Then I wrote Starz and Svetlana into the screenplay. I was writing everybody into the screenplay. But I felt bad for Starz, even though he'd stolen my girl. Starz didn't see what was coming, with the Count and Sylvia; he didn't sense the finality of what was going to go down, but I did. Sylvia would marry the Count, Starz's allowance would be cut off, and we would be evicted.

That was how we ended up working at the Seven Seas,

Starz and me, in the scullery. The dish room was called the scullery because the owner, Norm, Sylvias's ex, was retired Navy. It was damned decent of Norm to hire us on, but the work in the scullery was brutal with only three dishwashers, Starz and me and our supervisor, a little beer keg of a man named Joe Gorsky. Joe Gorsky was four and a half feet tall, full of muscle, and he was mad for work. His hands had only three fingers on them, and he had a speech defect of some sort. "*Guhh beg ahr guhh huhmm*," he'd shout. "Go big or go home!" As runty and deformed as he was, Joe Gorsky was a natural leader. There was something heroic about the man. He'd been toiling in the scullery for fourteen years and apparently he'd loved every minute of it. Charisma is a hard thing to pin down, but Joe Gorsky had it in spades. His esprit de corps was contagious and it spurred me on to work like a demon. "*Ugghh ugh mugh in dagh pugh pan roooom bughhugh*," he told me one day when Starz was out sick. "Just you and me in the pot and pan room, baby!"

Starz and I were sinking lower and lower. We were sleeping on Joe Gorsky's floor. This wasn't Paris poor, the romantic poverty of idealistic young artists, it was real poverty, third world poverty, the deep-night desolation that creeps in on rat's feet and shreds your soul. You get down too far, you lose your edge, that wafer-thin buffer zone that separates the human being from the beasts, and the street comes looking for you. You start out eating veal scaloppini in a Malibu beach house and you wind up living in a cardboard box on San Julian Street.

Starz was losing his grip. The paranoia was getting worse. He was seeing the soldier in tan cammies everywhere. It had to do with the drinking, of course. Then too he and Svetlana were dropping double stacks of X every night. He was constantly talking about the glory days in Hollywood. "I played ping pong with Gene Hackman on the set of *The Royal Tenenbaums*," he'd mutter fiercely as he wrestled with a charred sauté pan. "I pissed in Carrie Fisher's bathroom." He'd go on and on too about the lunch with Danny DeVito and Naomi Watts which he finally admitted took place not just the other day but back in 2005. On top of that, he wanted to go back to the beach house and cut down the six-foot San Pedro cactus and extract the mescaline. The end product would be worth around two G's on the street, he assured me. We'd need chemicals, sodium hydroxide and benzene... I didn't like the sound of it.

"By the way, do you have the ending yet?" he asked me one day when we were elbow deep in dirty dishes.

"The ending? The ending of what?"

"Of the screenplay."

"Maybe. The exorcist tries to escape in a boat and she fires the magic arrow into his heart and the boat bursts into flames..."

"A Viking funeral."

"Yeah, sort of."

"Bring it."

I was over Svetlana, but I met another Russian girl at Las Palmas. Katrinka. Katrinka wanted a hundred bucks, but I talked her down to seventy-five that I'd managed to borrow from Joe Gorsky. We went to a by-the-hour hotel on San Julian. She got silly drunk—on purpose, it seemed to me. She flopped around, consumed with laughter. Then she began weeping like a goat and talking Russian. I was pretty sure it was all an act. It was her sly way of spoiling a hard-on. But I was determined. Just the same, it was over in minutes. I was furious. Now she wanted to talk about Tolstoy. "You're disappointed," she chirped triumphantly. "Tell me something. I'm curious. Just what is it that you want from a woman, anyway?"

That was an easy one.

"A pleasant show of enthusiasm," I said.

Then Starz was picked up on a public drunk charge that turned into a 5150. A nurse called the restaurant from the psycho ward on Beverly. I got Starz out of there but he was thrashed. "I pissed in Carrie Fisher's bathroom," he kept saying. "I pissed in Carrie Fisher's bathroom."

After a few more days at the scullery we both decided that Starz would be better off in the nuthouse. "It's three hots and a cot," I prattled glibly. As soon as I'd handed Starz over to the nurse at the lunatic asylum I began to breathe easier. At least his hash was settled. I'd survive one way or another, I figured.

A Viking funeral... "My God, it's beautiful," I muttered to myself the next day as I scraped some glazed-on guck off a six pan. "She fires the magic arrow into his heart and the boat bursts into flames..."

2

Marlena's photograph has turned black. I no longer think about her every day, but when I do, there once again yawns beneath my feet an Auschwitz of despair. Her voice, when I hear it in my mind, has the quality of children's laughter echoing across a bomb crater. Her warmth is light years from me now, and I know it. I know it in my heart and in my soul. A part of me has been cut away forever by a scalpel. It's an operation in which I have been both the surgeon and the victim.

I loved Marlena beyond all boundaries of reason and passion. For her, I would gladly have become a regular guy—job, benefits, 401k, mortgage, car payments, credit cards, the works. She said she loved my lovemaking. As if I were a Shetland pony. "I want you back in my life," she told me. Sure, she wanted me in her life—sandwiched in between her low-impact aerobics and her nail appointments and her new husband and her fucking real estate deals. It was she who should have been the writer and I the realtor. How deftly she sketched the details of the vague but rosy future we'd share once she'd wrenched free from her impossible entanglements. Europe again, together, a second honeymoon. Venice, Florence, Paris. We'd live in the grand hotels and she'd dictate to me day and night. Our next book... We'd meander once again down the *Romantische Strasse* and make love all night in Schloss Neuschwanzstein. All lies, a grandiose pastiche splashed on a naked canvas with vague, careless strokes of a loose floppy brush—but cunningly, deftly, unerringly.

She had me going, the treacherous, conniving bitch. I swallowed it—all and everything. I believed her lies, I believed them explicitly, and today, even knowing what I know now, I would do it again. I would believe her lies even more explicitly, I'd beg her to confound me, to deceive me, I'd lick the lies from her lips, I would make her lies my catechism, my pledge of allegiance, my Lord's Prayer. I'd memorize her lies from A to Z, I'd repeat them in my sleep like a talking dog. I would do anything— anything—to hold her warm body in my arms one more time, to bury my face between her legs and kiss that beautiful furry treasure of hers, polluted though it was by the little man with the big bankroll and the shriveled legs. That invalid, that *half-man!* Her husband... But his prick still worked, the bastard!

But why should I kid myself? I was never anything more to Marlena than an amusement. Her new husband couldn't fuck her the way she wanted to be fucked so I was called in, like a relief pitcher who comes to the mound to put out a fire. And I put out the fire, by Jesus, and then I stoked it, and I put it out again. I was a good little Shetland pony for my goddamn high-assed nymphomaniac bitch. She got her precious orgasms, and when she was glutted with pleasure she pulled me out of herself and wiped me off with a Kleenex and tossed me into a dresser drawer stuffed with real estate contracts and aerobics schedules and squashed tubes of KY jelly. I was nothing more than a dildo to her, a rubber dick, a penis with a man attached.

Our third trip to Europe, this time to retrace our honeymoon tour. The flight from LA to Paris, we're over Pittsburgh now, and she's beside me with her bourbon old-fashioned, three cherries and two orange slices, and everything's ducky or so I imagine in my blissful innocence. Down below, Troy Hill, Pittsburgh's German-town, Marlena's birthplace. After a long snooze we cross the English Channel at dawn, then, after the endless descent to DeGaulle, we check into our hotel. A delirious tour of luminous, lamp-lit Paris, retracing our honeymoon, the same restaurants, the same bistros, even the bench under the trees on the *Boulevard de Clichy* where Henri Charriere sat in 1967 and looked back over his life after finally escaping from French Guyana and writing *Papillon*.

Then over to Montparnasse, the *rue de la Gaité*, where we lose each other accidentally-on-purpose and *he's* there, *him*, the little man with the shriveled legs and the big bucks. Back at the hotel, a note: "Sorry..." My beautiful bird has flown, taking with her most of the money, and I'm back on Papi's bench on the *Boulevard de Clichy*, with an airplane ticket, my hotel vouchers and less than a hundred francs in my pocket.

*T*he jacaranda trees on Wilshire are shedding their delicate lavender bells. I took the dog for a walk. I haven't given her a name. Why should I? Would you give a beetle a name? Or a bedbug?

Cliff English, my editor at Pompeii Press, says I have an unfortunate tendency to inject humor into my work. The readers don't want humor, he says. Well, fuck the readers! I don't like writing BDSM. But I don't like busing tables either. My painter pal Byron Lovelace says I'm prostituting myself to the "plutocrat capitalist pigs." But in my life, some of my best friends have been prostitutes. Most of them, in fact. I prefer the word "whores," incidentally, to "prostitutes." It has a Biblical ring.

Fausto came to my door this morning with a book, *The*

Labyrinth of Solitude, by Octavio Paz, and several bottles of *Château de Puligny-Montrachet*. The wine was a gift from one of his fans, a tarnished diva from Pacific Palisades who claims she's read every one of Fausto's charming Fernando de León books. She bought him a whole case of the stuff.

In the early days—back in the 20th century—when Fausto and I shared a loft in the warehouse district and I was in love with Suzy Soojian, an Armenian girl who worked at the Kosher Burrito in Little Tokyo, we used to watch reruns of old Fernando Lamas movies on TV—including his early Argentinean films such as *En El Ultimo Piso*, as well as the American splash-extravaganzas of the 50's in which the iconic lady killer—suave, sweetly dangerous—seduces million dollar mermaids in an Olympic size pools—and Fausto often remarked that Fernando Lamas was his exact double. It's true. Fausto looks more like Fernando Lamas than Fernando Lamas.

"Wine and solitude," Fausto assured me as he cracked open a bottle of the *Puligny-Montrachet*. "That's all a writer needs, my friend. Wine and solitude."

"Bullshit!" That's what I told Fausto. I've tried the wine and solitude bit—months of it, years even—and all it ever did was make me lonely and drunk. But I have to say that Octavio Paz's title, "*The Labyrinth of Solitude*" perfectly describes this crumbling old hotel.

After Paris, after Marlena, it was primarily an interior life I was living here on Sonrisa Street, in the Labyrinth of Solitude. The more I remained in the womblike world of my cell the more intense my torpor became. I lived a symbolic life, lying on my bunk listening to the voices that came through the walls. I curled up like a flower, like the uroborus, the fabulous serpent that swallows its own tail. I fell into a vegetative stupor. I didn't know whether I would come back or not. I didn't care. I began to live the life of a mineral or a rock. The tiniest event could amuse me for hours, even though I no longer had any concept of hours or even of time. In the gurgle of water dripping from the broken tap down the hall and the rustle of curtains fanned by the breeze I discovered strange contingencies and unheard-of relationships. The sound of a branch tapping on the windowpane sent me into raptures, and when I heard through my cell wall the subdued hum and chatter of the ancient elevator ascending in the depths of the hive I was in heaven. I spent hours staring at the hairline cracks in the plaster. A flyspeck, when I fixed it with my hypnagogic gaze, blossomed into a riot of myth. And if a fat cockroach scampered across my field of vision it was an event no less momentous than the Second Coming of Christ.

Then there was the Man on the Other Side of the Wall. The Man on the Other Side of the Wall was perfectly real, yet I never saw him because he never ventured out of his room. He had his groceries sent up. The Yellow Cab brought them. He, the Man on the Other Side of the Wall, kept me awake night after night with his ranting and raving. His voice was hoarse and gruff, often edged with tears. I pictured him as an old man grappling with phantoms from the past. He was pouring out an endless tirade of anger and remorse. I imagined him kneeling by his bunk, like a penitent in his cell. Sometimes he'd pound on the floor, sob, and bellow like a steer. Or he'd roar in an evangelical voice, words I couldn't comprehend. Maybe he was talking in tongues for all I know. It would go on, Biblical-like, for hours, then suddenly he'd interrupt himself with—"*Hazel's home from the hospital, Mama! Everything's all right now!*" Or: "*Here, kitty, kitty, kitty!*" Frequently, as he went through his machinations, I heard the clunk of a heavy metal object banging on the floorboards. It figured to be a gun...

3

*F*austo's got it! Spiritual gonorrhea: a sort of syphilis of the soul. Small wonder. Everyone has it. The disease is universal, at least in the 21st century. It's not despair that's eating Fausto away, but ennui.

I drop by his apartment to cheer him up. Sunk deep in an overstuffed chair, wearing a white undershirt—*so Latin*—Fausto leafs listlessly through the pages of *Cosmic Consciousness*, by Richard Maurice Bucke.

"This book was once food and drink to me," he murmurs. "Now I can't look at it..."

Such world-weariness! His voice seems to be coming from inside a bathyscaph submerged miles deep on the ocean floor. He's talking in fish-syllables, his voice warped by the inconceivable weight of the water.

"Once I had a thirst for knowledge. Freud's Eros and Thanatos, Jung's Archetypes. What are the lineaments of the soul? During my student days in Prague we'd often stay up all night discussing these subjects. What happens to the soul after death? Is there such a thing as reincarnation? What is cosmic consciousness? What is nirvana? What is samadhi? How does one attain it? The Hindus speak of a state in which the ears have opened to the song of the universe, and the eyes to the radiant mind of God. Is it true that when the pupil is ready, the master appears? I was vitally interested in all this stuff. I lived in a world of books, a world of ideas. And these ideas were tremendously stimulating. My head was in the clouds, my feet scarcely brushing the ground. You may not believe this, Donaldo, but I was once very shy, very withdrawn. I had to learn to be mundane. To make a stupid remark, to say a foolish thing, anything, in order to...get in touch..."

I'm smiling because as Fausto lets loose this phrase, "I had to learn to be mundane," I seem to see him descending from the clouds like a paratrooper, devouring everything with his tiny greedy black eyes, ready to take the world by storm, itching to plunder its cities, its riches, its women.

He's going on now. He became mundane, and now he's so goddamn mundane he can't stand himself. Where now is the fire? Where's the fever? Where did it go?

I feel I have to say something, so I interrupt his monologue: "My friend, surely a man of your intelligence—"

"Donaldo, I've waited so long to hear you say that... My intelligence. Yes! It was my intelligence, from the beginning, after all, that set me apart from the others. You know my background, my friend. I speak six languages! I was a racing driver, I was a soccer star—*fútbol!* I was an actor. But look what I have become. A writer. A paperback writer. A paper man. *Un hombre de papel...*"

Fausto has a tremendous nostalgia for the old days, the Bareback Books days. And with good reason too. We were both sitting pretty back then, back in the 20th century. It was a very fertile period, the Bareback Books period. I was "Orgasmo"—yes, I was Orgasmo—and Fausto was "Fernando de León." The pay was abysmally low of course, but you got advances. We were poor, yes. We weren't bucks up. That's not what I meant when I said we were sitting pretty. Fausto was driving a taxi in order to make ends meet, and I was busting suds at Clifton's Silver Spoon.

"Los Angeles is the theater of our destiny."

That's what Norma Jacoby, our editor at Bareback Books, used to say to us, Fausto and me, when we had our story conferences at the Hollywood Gorky's on Cahuenga over Russian beers and borsht with cabbage and sour cream. It's true that Norma Jacoby had a tendency to pontificate, especially when she was half in the bag, and we'd laugh, Fausto and I, at the "theater of our destiny" business, but at the same time we believed it, at least at some level. It wasn't about the money. There was sense of shared optimism, a sense that everything was still up ahead of us, that something truly magical was going to happen, right around the next corner. I don't know how to explain it. Maybe it was the last gasp of our youth, who can say?

During this period I was doing three paperback titles a month for Bareback Books. I got a penny a word. In order to make a minimal living I had to crank out 130,000 words a month, or about 7,000 words a day. One thing this regimen taught me about writing was to shoot first and ask questions later. At a penny a word you don't anguish over nuances. You become one with the computer, driving forward always, no pauses, no deliberation, no hesitation, and when you're really on, the words are in your fingers, not in your head, and that's the joy of it, if one may speak of joy as a component of such drudgery.

Because Norma Jacoby frequently threw rewrites my way, I became familiar with the work of some of the other Bareback writers. Bareback's straight or heterosexual line, Bareback Bedtime Books, was dominated by myself—Orgasmo—and J. W. Hanlon, a youngster from Thomasville, Georgia, "the Kid from Thomasville," as Norma called him.

The Kid from Thomasville was a heavy edit. He couldn't spell and he didn't know punctuation.

Nevertheless he delivered copy and plenty of it. This courageous young man was trying to support a wife and three kids by cranking out porn at the rate of up to six titles a month. That's 10,000 words a day. But the crotch novels were merely a means of earning money. Like me, like Fausto, the Kid from Thomasville was trying to be a "real" writer. So after his daily 10,000-word stint for Bareback Books he would tackle his own work, a post-Faulknerian deep-south novel dealing with intermarried rural families, and then in the pre-dawn hours, long after most men would have collapsed, he pounded out desperately earnest letters—to me, to Norma Jacoby, and to Ruby Fine, owner and publisher of Bareback Books—setting forth his intentions, ambitions and ideas about writing. That was how I learned about the Kid's personal life—through correspondence.

One thing I know. This guy was a Writer, with a capital W. This is not your Guggenheim Fellowship man, anguishing over sugarcoated nuances. This is a man worried about the rent, about groceries, about utilities, cranking out his payload every day to keep the bill collector away from the door and then diving headlong into his own work with the guts of a football linebacker. When it comes to guts this man beats everybody.

Among my most excruciating tasks at Bareback Books were the hatchet jobs I had to do on manuscripts that were submitted by earnest unknown literary writers. These misguided submissions were eagerly pounced upon and assessed by Norma Jacoby and Bareback publisher Ruby Fine. Could this book—"substantially revised"—appeal to our readers? That was the question. The reason Ruby Fine and Norma Jacoby preferred these books was because they already had the structure, plot, intensity, realness—life—to make a good go on the market once the "hot scenes" were spliced in.

That was my job. I was in charge of cutting the heart out of these naive and hopeful writers' books and injecting the necessary hot scenes. The authors were advised in a form letter that their manuscripts were accepted pending "substantial revisions." Little did they dream what kind of a mangling their manuscripts would receive. When I got through with my dirty work their books read more like a nocturnal emission than a novel. I don't know what else to say at this juncture except to repeat Dostoevsky's words to a young student, "To write well one must suffer, suffer!"

Our gay line, Lesbos Literary Classics, was written exclusively by Ruby Fine under the name of Lila Nero. Ruby Fine would allow no one but Norma Jacoby to touch her Lila Nero manuscripts.

Ruby Fine was a fat frog of a woman whose fat fingers sparkled with fat diamonds. Her favorite dress was a bile-green muumuu with a gauzy sheen that reminded me of tainted meat or curdled urine. Her forearms were covered with coarse black hair, and her face, comically magnified by thick glasses, was the face of a greedy pollywog. Her expression seemed to say: *This is my world, little man. While you are in it, you will obey my commandments.*

Norma Jacoby was a capable editor and a savvy businesswoman. She'd spent a decade as a newspaper reporter in Honolulu. Norma had literary aspirations. For years she'd been trying to finish a novel called "Beyond the Burma Road." Norma had grown up in Burma after World War II, the granddaughter of an American fighter pilot and a beautiful, artistic half-Chinese woman. "Beyond the Burma Road" was the story of her youth, adolescence and first love, with the war and her dashing flyer grandfather's career as a backdrop. I'd read parts of "Beyond the Burma Road" and it was potentially a good book, a real book, written from the guts, and yet there was something about it that was too facile, too fluent, too palatable, too readable.

It was Norma's newspaper experience that had ruined her style. That's my opinion. She had a tendency to encapsulate, to homogenize, to reduce everything to a common denominator, to the excruciating banality of the daily headlines. The slush she edited out was the very stuff she should have left in. I mean the raw albumen that sticks to the pages, the tentative flames of thought that shoot across the horizon then flicker and gutter out, the leering, crooked streets that lead nowhere, the blind alleys, the dead ends, the sudden glimpses of flashing wings that speak of aborted flights. I'm sure the book would have been published if she could have finished it. I even knew what the critics would say: "Two thumbs up! Long overdue. *Beyond the Burma Road* is a story that desperately needed to be told. An indispensable book..."

But that's just it. "Beyond the Burma Road" was one of those indispensable books with which one can quite easily dispense.

Pompeii Press, Bareback's bondage line, was authored primarily by a retired Marine colonel who lived in Cardiff-by-the-Sea. I did a few Pompeii titles myself under the name of Hal Harrelson. The Pompeii books were far more interesting to do than the Bedtime line because of the exotic settings and the nasty tricks of the villains. There were no villains in the Bedtime books, only tireless, faceless protagonists, and the action, as decreed by company policy, went down in such Meccas of drabness as Smallville, Littletown, Middlevale and Centerville. The Pompeii formula was different, but quite simple: an affluent, white American woman from Beverly Hills, La Jolla or Laguna Nigel was whisked away to some far-flung locale where she was ravished by fierce, muscular, dark-skinned men, typically Arabs, Turks or Ethiopians.

One of my Pompeii books, set in Haiti, garnered a shitload of fan mail from readers, due to the unexpected popularity of a minor character, Malvolio, a dwarf jailer with an enormous penis. Norma herself was so taken with Malvolio that she wrote a series of books under the name of Jackie LaPrix, which she published in the Bedtime line, starring my character, renamed "the Dirty Little Dwarf."

How very like Norma it was to take a primordial, atavistic character like Malvolio, a figure fairly dripping with the green and gold of the unconscious, and transport him—sanitized, standardized and furnished with a white skin—to the tepid birdbath-world of Centerville, Smallville and Middlevale. Titles? *The Dirty Little Dwarf Goes to College, The Dirty Little Dwarf Surfs Naked,* etc.

Ruby Fine's husband was a big-time lawyer. It was he who bankrolled the publishing company. Bareback Books was Ruby's toy and a vehicle for her lesbian "classics." A writer she wasn't, Ruby Fine, but she did know business. She made money. For the writers, of course, it was a different story. She squeezed her writers dry. She had us jumping through our ass while she raked it in. Repeatedly she promised to put us, Fausto and me, on a royalties contract instead of the standard humiliating "author for hire" agreement, but it never happened. Several of my books went into multiple printings, too. I could have cleaned up.

Now an hour has passed and Fausto is listlessly turning the pages of *Cosmic Consciousness* once again, still sunk deep in his chair, still sunk in gloom, and he's still going on about the *hombre de papel* business and how he's lost his soul and all. Fausto's a great pal, but he's a tricky bastard too, and I can't help recalling how, more than a decade ago, he inveigled me into finishing up his dog novel, *Doberman's Delight,* while he flew off to Rio for an extended holiday with a Colombian coffee baroness. That would have been okay, but Fausto didn't return and he didn't return and I was stuck doing Canine Classics. I did all right, too, if I do say so myself. Once again, within the narrow confines of the prescribed format I displayed originality and panache. In *Passionate Puppies,* my first title after *Doberman's Delight,* I created a character that grabbed the readers by the balls—an astonishingly vigorous, three-year-old black-and-tan Doberman pinscher named Sultan. Immediately, the fan mail began pouring in and sales figures soared. *Passionate Puppies* was followed by *Sultan's Sweet Urge* and *Sultan's Sex Secret*, both big sellers, and *Sultan's Savage Sex Slave* was an even bigger hit. Norma was beside herself and even Ruby Fine was impressed with my prowess. I was carrying Canine Classics single-handedly.

The upshot of all this was that when Fausto finally dragged back in from Rio he wormed his way into my spot as prime mover in the Bedtime Books Series and I, thanks to my roaring success, became the reluctant kingpin of the dog novels.

I thought I'd hit rock bottom with Canine Classics, but not too long after this the shit really hit the fan. Ruby Fine caught me recycling my manuscripts. I'd take one of my previous books, shuffle the scenes around, change the names of the characters, and bingo. I got by with it for quite a while before she caught on. I thought she was going to fire me, but instead she put Fausto back in his old spot at Canine Classics and she banished me to the Pompeii line.

Still, we were happy, relatively happy, Fausto and I, back in the old days, the Bareback Books days. I was Orgasmo and Fausto was Fernando de León.

The ancient Greeks told tales of a Golden Age when man and beast spoke the same tongue and people lived like deer in a forest. Heroes and maidens danced with nymphs and satyrs to the music of Pan's pipes and drank spring wine from crystal goblets. The Golden Age ended when Prometheus stole fire from the gods and taught men to be clever, and each succeeding age—Silver, Bronze, Iron—signaled a steady deterioration in the quality of life as men grew more and more clever, more and more sophisticated, more and more civilized.

The Bareback Books period, back in the 20th century, that was my Golden Age. Then came the 21st century and the digital revolution and everything turned to shit. Norma Jacoby takes over the reins at Pompeii Press and Bareback Books becomes a mere repository for out-of-print crotch novels. Then, drunk with power, Norma hired Cliff English on as managing editor and changed Pompeii Press to a website, ebooks, electronic copies only. No print copies and no bookstore presence. And no more advances for the Pompeii writers.

Welcome to the 21st century. The great god Pan is dead!

4

I ran into my old friend Byron Lovelace the painter the other day down at Arco Plaza. Byron's an Abstract Expressionist but he makes a precarious living copying old masters. He'd just sold a painting, another copy of Leonardo's *Last Supper*, and he was in a jubilant mood.

"Come on," he chirped, "I'm taking you to lunch."

Byron's cracked glasses frames are bound together with grimy adhesive tape. He seldom takes a bath. On a hot day the stink of the man is enough to knock a horse down. Byron lives with his mother in Westlake.

We go La Golondrina, a tourist trap on Olvera Street, which is fine with me because La Golondrina is the sort of place where you meet the big bouncy blondes from Minnesota who've come to southern California to get their business fixed.

The restaurant is crowded but we're seated immediately on the whitewashed brick patio. There's a Minnesota blonde at the next table. Byron orders the house chenin blanc. After we've blurred the edges a little bit we order the *costillas en adobo*, and Byron calls for more wine. "The first thing an artist should learn is how to use a gun," he says. The Minnesota blonde is giving me the eye over the rim of her margarita glass, and I'm beginning to feel that maybe life can be beautiful after all.

As Byron and I are toasting his latest sale, Sol Fingerbein and a woman roughly the size of a small rhinoceros are being shown to a table. Sol Fingerbein is clinging fiercely to the rhinoceros-woman's arm, but he appears to be perched on her shoulder.

"The first thing an artist should learn is how to use a gun," Byron repeats. Donald? Donald, are you listening?"

"Yeah, sure...yes..."

"My friend, there are four ways for an artist to survive in this world. One, be born with a silver spoon in your mouth; two, marry a rich girl; three, get yourself a nice clean war wound."

"And the fourth?"

"Use a gun. Walk into a bank with a piece of iron in your fist and demand the cash. I read an article in the paper this morning. Some desperado held up a bank on La Cienega. Strolled out with half a million berries. Think of it! The robber blew a teller away in the process, the paper said. What the fuck! Is that so bad? Killing one person? A painter has to eat, doesn't he? Maybe it's right that some little bank teller should die or spend the rest of his life in a fucking wheelchair so that I can do my work without worrying about where my next meal is coming from. Let me ask you this: how do you ever expect to do your own work when you're writing day and night for Pompeii Press? Maybe it's time you took a good look at yourself, buddy boy! For fuck's sake, Donald, do you realize what you are? You're a *pornographer!*"

"Byron, your paintings are selling. Listen to me. You got 200 bucks for this last job—"

"Right, right. You're absolutely right. That's the third sale this month, in fact."

The Minnesota blonde departs and the *costillas en adobo* arrive, garnished with pineapple rings, cilantro and pickled slices of red onion. Byron pulls his tattered spiral notebook out of his shirt pocket. He puts on his glasses and thumbs through the greasy pages

"Yeah, here we are... I sold two in June, two in May, three in April... Let's see, that's sixteen *Last Suppers* since March. And eleven *Mona Lisas*. My total for last year was twenty-seven *Last Suppers* and fourteen *Mona Lisas*. Not bad, you say, but what does it do for me, except keep me alive? It's not my work, don't you understand that? Look beyond your nose! Look beyond your stomach, if you can, for once in your life. It's all copies of fucking Leonardo. I tell you, Donald, it's time to bury Leonardo and Michelangelo and the rest of those shits. Botticelli, Verrocchio, Tintoretto, Caravaggio, Paolo Uccello. *Fuck those wops!* Let them fade gracefully into the chiaroscuro where they belong. Let the dead bury their dead. They've had their day. Now it's our day. It's time, I'm telling you. It's time!"

I'd been hoping, after we'd finished the meal, that Byron would order more wine. And then maybe another wave of Minnesota blondes would arrive, and things would start to happen. But instead Byron glanced at his watch, then abruptly hopped to his feet and excused himself. He was off to trade massages with Derek Delmonico, a young pastel artist who lives in West Hollywood.

It's not that Byron is gay. But a woman would be hoping for too much.

This morning the Gypsy Lady knocked at my door wanting to borrow an onion. Moments later I heard crazy laughter so I stuck my head out again. One of the midgets was turning cartwheels in the hallway. And I smelled sauerkraut. I think the Gypsy Lady is making *székely gulyás*.

Byron dropped by. It had been a month since our lunch at La Golondrina. We took the bus downtown. Byron was excited; he'd just sold another copy of the *Mona Lisa*, but it turned out that there was something else he wanted to talk to me about.

"Guess what," he began, as we were crossing Bonnie Brae Street, "*I'm* writing a novel. Does that surprise you?"

"Not at all. Why should it? If you can paint you can write."

We go to Clifton's and find an out of the way table. We both get the split pea soup and the cornbread. Byron is bursting with talk about his book.

"*Whom The Gods Love!* That's the title. Do you like it?" Without waiting for my reply he goes on: "The hero's name is Marcus Maduke. That's one of the pen names you used when you wrote for Bareback Books. Isn't that right? The truth is, I've chosen you as the model for the lead character. He's a middle-aged writer with a suitcase full of rejected novels, unknown, unpublished, a complete failure. You don't mind my saying that, do you? It all goes back to something we talked about that day at La Golondrina. We were sitting on the patio, remember? *The first thing an artist should learn is how to use a gun.* Well, that was just a germ, a nucleus. This thing has grown, believe me! My head is seething with ideas. I understand how it is with you guys now, you writers. You get an idea in your head, and you go crazy with it. It takes over your life. Ideas are an obsession, a drug. Not a drug that brings you down, a drug that puts you to sleep, but a snort of pure oxygen—a sort of intellectual cocaine. Do you like that phrase, 'intellectual cocaine?' Listen, I've got a million of 'em. The minute I started jotting down ideas for this book I felt something click. Let's take, for example, my choice of the name for the lead character, Marcus Maduke. It's perfect, don't you see? And my other characters: Lloyd Masselin, Karen Mulhern, Tessa Tremaine. I'm finding that I have a knack for that, for choosing character names. This facility of mine—and I hope I don't appear too self-congratulatory—is something I find lacking in your work, if you don't mind a shot of criticism from an old friend. For example, your book about Mexico that was never published. What was the title? *Tarantula Woman?* There was that fat girl—the whore who was supposedly in love with you. What was her name? Profunda, ah, yes, Profunda. Somehow that didn't ring true..."

"That was her real name. I didn't bother to change it because I knew she'd never read the book. She couldn't read. She was illiterate."

"Ah, yes. Her real name. I understand now. But it wasn't 'real' real. Know what I mean?"

"No."

What I like about Clifton's Cafeteria is that it reminds me of the cafeteria in New York that Isaac Singer describes so beautifully in his books, a place where he and other destitute writers subsisted on bowls of noodles and coffee cake—and conversation. I can almost see him, Isaac Bashevis Singer, sitting a few tables away, a frail but luminous figure, writing in Yiddish, a bowl of noodles at his elbow, his head percolating, now pausing to reflect, now lost in thought, now writing furiously, his electric blue eyes snapping as the words migrate from his head to his fingertips like a swarm of bees.

"Let's get back to the plot," Byron is saying. "I think you'll find this interesting. Marcus Maduke—we'll call him Marc—has a painter friend, Lloyd Masselin, modeled of course on yours truly. Lloyd counsels Marc. He has a sure-fire scheme, you see, for getting published. The conversation goes something like this:

"'Listen to me, Marc. The way to publication is fame. The way to fame is crime. Commit a spectacular crime and you become a world figure. Get media exposure and publication is assured. Get your manuscripts in order, buy a gun with a telescopic sight and grab a plane to Washington—or a taxi to Hollywood. It doesn't matter whether you kill the President or a princess or a movie star. As long as it's somebody famous. That's your ticket, Marc. Publication guaranteed. They'll probably make a movie about you, too—like they did with Lee Harvey

Oswald and Gary Gilmore and Charlie Manson and the Boston Strangler. The criminal celebrity Caryl Chessman wrote the best seller, *Cell 2455, Death Row,* while awaiting execution at San Quentin. Did you know that? James Earl Ray, convicted murderer of Martin Luther King, presently pursues a burgeoning literary career from his cell at the River Bend Penitentiary in Nashville. Mark David Chapman, John Lennon's assassin, signed a book contract shortly after being imprisoned at Attica and even wrote to Yoko Ono to ask that she participate in the venture. Incidentally, Chapman had with him when he shot Lennon outside the Dakota a copy of *The Catcher in the Rye*—not a bad book, by the way—a circumstance which reaffirms an association I've been investigating, the close connection, in modern times, between literature and crime, between literature and murder, and in particular, between literature and assassination.'

"I also want to mention in this context something I unearthed about John Wilkes Booth, Lincoln's assassin. It seems that Booth gave a sealed letter to the actor John Mathews—to be delivered to the publishers of the *National Intelligencer*—this on the day of the assassination. The letter, which was never published, since Mathews burned it, explained how Booth had devoted his time, money and energies to arranging President Lincoln's kidnapping, all without success, and that it was now time to take more definitive action. The delivery of the letter to Mathews was followed by the shooting at the Ford Theater, the flight of John Wilkes Booth to Zekiah Swamp and his demise at the Garret Farmhouse.

"'Well,' Lloyd Masselin goes on, 'you see what I'm getting at, Marc, my boy. Put your manuscripts in order, buy yourself a gun, select a famous victim, pull the trigger... You're made! Beautiful, isn't it? I imagine they'll let you go on writing in prison, too—unless you get the chair. Either way, you win.'

"*The first thing an artist should learn is how to use a gun.* Do you get it now? So, Marc decides to take Lloyd's advice. After all, life is war. He'll blow some celebrity away in order to pull himself up into the spotlight on the coat tails of a famous corpse. And so the die is cast.

"The rest of the plot is rather elementary. Having decided on a course of action, Marc sets about his work with elaborate precision. He packs his thirteen rejected novels in a steamer trunk and places the trunk in storage. He drafts a 'Letter of Explanation,' a document that tells quite candidly why he did what he did, and he dispatches the letter to his attorney along with the key to the storage unit where his manuscripts are held. Accompanying the sealed Letter of Explanation and the key are instructions to his attorney stating that the contents of the sealed envelope are to be released simultaneously to the police and to the press when Marc is arrested or upon notification of his death.

"Marc's plan, incidentally, is to assassinate the President of the United States. He buys a folding rifle with a telescopic sight, practices at a range, and makes several trips to Washington for dry runs. In the meantime, he begins a diary—'The Assassination Diary'—documenting his preparations, his thoughts, his misgivings, his resolutions, and so on. Never before has an assassin provided the world at large with so thorough an examination of his motives, and of the living, thinking mind behind those motives. The Assassination Diary, Marc realizes, is a human document of the utmost importance. He is filled now with a sense of purpose, a sense of destiny. What was it Napoleon said? 'I feel myself driven towards an end that I do not know. As soon as I shall have reached it, an atom will suffice to shatter me. Till then, not all the forces of mankind can do anything against me.'

"I know I'm doing all the talking," Byron interrupts himself. "Would you like another bowl of soup? What about some cornbread? I hope I'm not boring you."

"No, no, no, no..."

"The rest of the plot, as I say, is elementary. After the dry runs and the preparations, comes at last the real thing. Marc flies to Washington for his rendezvous with destiny. He makes his way to the roof of a building that he has previously reconnoitered, a vantage point from which he'll have a clear shot at the President's caravan when it passes, as he has previously ascertained, at three that afternoon. He has with him, in addition to the murder weapon, The Assassination Diary, in which he's madly scribbling. He has made a pact with himself to record his thoughts and actions right up the decisive moment when he squeezes the trigger, and beyond, until he surrenders himself to the arms of the police. As the hour approaches, however, a seemingly unrelated incident transpires. A prostitute and her pimp have also ascended to the roof, and are involved in a violent altercation. The pimp slaps the woman around. She's sobbing, and her face is covered in blood. Marc, outraged, rushes to the conflict and tries to protect the woman, and in the process he's stabbed and fatally wounded by the pimp.

"The pimp and the prostitute rush off, leaving Marc to die. The President's caravan passes without incident, and Marc bleeds to death on the concrete. As an ironic footnote, at this very moment Marc's agent telephones to inform him that one of his novels, *The Brass Lollypop*, has just been accepted for publication."

Byron pauses for a moment, dangling his spoon over his soup, and for an hallucinating instant I see Isaac Singer with the tablets in his hands and the words shooting like flames from his fingertips.

"Well, what do you think of it? I admit that it's based, to some extent, on *Crime and Punishment*. Why not? Raskolnikov killed the old pawnbroker, Lizaveta, to prove that he was a man of action—a Napoleon. But Napoleon doesn't have to prove he's Napoleon, don't you see? Raskolnikov is very much like you and me. He's not a man of action, and he never will be. He's a Hitler without charisma. He's trapped inside the prison of his own mind. He's a failed artist, an angel without wings. In the end, it's Sonia, the 'holy prostitute' who provides the way to salvation. Inspired by his love for her, Raskolnikov moves out of the arena of the intellect altogether. He enters a new dimension for him—the realm of the spirit. In the same way, my hero, Marcus Maduke, alias you, the failed writer...he has it all planned out, the assassination of the President, but at the last instant, fate intervenes. He follows his heart. He moves to rescue the prostitute, a woman who is altogether unworthy of his attentions. But that doesn't matter, you see. What matters is his action— pure, unselfish...totally extraneous to the program he has set up for himself. And although it costs him his life, there is a sense of fulfillment, because he's come full circle, from alienation to involvement. Well, what do you..."

What do I think! My Christ! I'm astonished at Byron's description of his novel. My God, the man's a genius. A Picasso of literature! Why, I've never hatched anything remotely approaching *Whom the Gods Love!*

But a week went by and then two, and I found myself at Clifton's once again, thinking about Byron's novel. A sparkling précis, to be sure, Byron, but will you be able to write it? Haven't I listened to the dreams of an army corps of would-be writers, talking out their books in a hundred shit-hole bars? Great expectations, yes, but can you sit down at the typewriter and churn it out? Can you sit there hour after hour, until the words are no longer entities in your mind but flames leaping from your fingertips?

As if in answer to my question, in walked Byron, and he was flying high. He'd just sold a copy of Van Gogh's *Starry Night*. And the novel? *Whom the Gods Love?* What about the novel? He mumbled something about needing to do some more research and quickly changed the subject. Then he took his grubby spiral notebook out of his shirt pocket and began thumbing through the pages.

"Check it out," he burbled, "that's the third *Starry Night* this month! And listen to this, Donaldo. My total sales for the year so far are twelve *Starry Nights*, fifteen *Mona Lisas* and fourteen *Last Suppers*..."

5

*J*ust before Halloween I got a surprise package from Tuscany—my father's mandolin, mailed to me by my half sister Solange, whom I'd never met and of whose existence I'd only recently learned.

The story of my father's mandolin goes back to my childhood. I was six years old and the family was living in Cooperstown. My sister Erin must have been about five, and there was also an older girl who lived with us briefly. I don't think I ever knew her name. Erin and I called her the "Big Girl." The Big Girl was with us for a week, maybe less, and then she vanished.

One day I climbed the rickety stairs to the attic where I discovered my father's mandolin tucked away with some old picture frames and broken china. I carried the mandolin down to the kitchen where my mother was boiling noodles. I sat down on the kitchen floor and began, in my untutored child's way, to pluck the strings. My mother's reaction was swift and violent. She snatched the instrument out of my hands, smashed it by whacking it on the kitchen table, then crunched it over her knee and stuffed it in the trash. And the Big Girl, I remember, was peering around a corner, with a horrified look on her face.

"Don't you ever touch your father's mandolin again!" my mother snapped.

I guessed that I wouldn't, since it had already been destroyed and discarded.

The reason for my mother's violent opposition to my learning the mandolin or any musical instrument was that my father, in his early years, had been a traveling musician. I never knew any of this when I was a child. It was only many years later, near the time of my father's death, when I began to pry into the family secrets, that I learned something of his early history, and that my father had been married twice, and that, in fact, I had a half-sister, Solange, an artist of some repute who lived in Tuscany.

I paid a visit to Aunt Livia, my father's sister, at a trailer park in Sarasota Florida, and she filled me in on some of the details. My father, Rufus, had a wonderful singing voice, according to Aunt Liv, and he could play any stringed instrument. He formed a band, the Oneonta Muskrat Ramblers, and started out on the road. He married a beautiful torch singer named Margey Baxter and they began a musical career together. Margey was a very wild girl and they lived a reckless day-to-day life, and eventually Margey Baxter ran off with a drummer.

My father was crushed, and then, a short time later at a dance, Rufus met my mother, a stiff, puritanical woman who was the exact opposite of Margey Baxter, and she agreed to marry him if he would promise to give up the musician's life forever. And so Rufus undertook an "Act of Contrition." He reversed his field. He resolved to do the eight-to-five. And he did. He became a telephone lineman. I was born, and my sister Erin, and we lived a sedate and sterile life, under the aegis of my mother. The music was forgotten, in fact banished, and my father's mandolin, his only instrument that survived the purge, wound up in the attic gathering dust—until it was picked up by my chubby six year-old hand.

And the "Big Girl," Aunt Liv explained, was of course Solange. Margey Baxter, perpetually on the road, was unable to care for her daughter, so she sent the child to live with us. But my mother wasn't having any of it because in her mind Solange was a link to that wild life she'd made my father promise to leave behind. So my mother gave her would-be stepdaughter the bum's rush and Solange wound up at the Carrie Deakins Cobb Orphanage for Girls in Willow Grove Pennsylvania. But luck was with Solange. She was adopted by a wealthy Philadelphia couple, grew up rich, and studied art at Bryn Mawr, where her talent blossomed.

In a very chummy letter that accompanied the package from Tuscany Solange explained how she'd fished the broken mandolin out of the trash that day. She'd glued it back together as best she could, and she kept the mandolin with her at the orphanage as her only memento of the father who had abandoned her. Solange graciously invited me to visit her at her villa in Montefollononico for "as long as you like," and of course I would have gone in a heartbeat if I'd had the airfare, but the next morning over *café con leche* at La Pachanga, an out of the way dive near Lafayette Park, I wrote a warm and chatty letter, thanking Solange, and I promised to visit ASAP. I also asked her point blank, "Why did you send me the mandolin?" She wrote back, a week later: "It seemed like the right thing to do." And it was right, I think, because it was as if I'd picked up my father's life where he left off when he married my mother. His unlived life, I mean. I inherited the chaos, the roaring chaos, the confusion and the fiery longing, the unfulfilled destiny of an artist who was nipped in the bud, a musician who instead became a soldier in the bread-and-butter wars. Rufus settled for a comfortable death. In a sense he laid down his life for us, for Erin and myself. When I unwrapped the package and saw my father's mandolin after all those years, lovingly mended, restored and varnished, I knew why Solange had sent it to me. Rufus had forsaken his calling and the baton was passed to me. My father's mandolin was Excalibur. For better or for worse, I had pulled the sword out of the rock.

*L*a Pachanga was an interesting place back in the day, before the new owner came along. On the inside it wasn't much, just a few scabby tables scattered around an ancient mahogany bar that curled like a question mark and disappeared abruptly into a dark steamy kitchen reeking with beef tripe and garlic, but they did have an autographed celebrity poster on the wall next to the fire extinguisher, "Best chipotle sauce in town, Ray Liotta." Plus the food was hearty and the prices were cheap. The old owner was a Turk, horny as a monkey, and he wore a huge sparkler on each pinkie. Leticia, the skinny waitress, pretended to be fair game because she wanted to keep her job. In order to distract Mustafa she'd bring him street girls. She knew all the whores around Lafayette Park. Fortunately for Leticia, Mustafa spent a lot of time trying to poison the two feral cats that lived in the avocado tree out by the dumpster. Those cats were something. You'd see the pair of them ranging over the rooftops. Both were black but one had a white paw. They'd raid the dumpster every day. Roderick, a homeless philosophy professor, used to save them scraps from his *huevos rancheros* in the morning. Roderick was on a tab at La Pachanga. He'd pay up every once in a while when his veteran's check came in. He had a nice little hooch he'd built out by the dumpster. It wasn't cardboard. It was made out of branches and sticks woven together and wrapped up with chicken wire and twine, like an oriole's nest.

It was beautiful the way Roderick had everything fixed up back there, his razor hanging on a string from the avocado tree along with a fragment of mirror glass, his socks dangling from a little clothesline, his tiny smooth bar of soap in a plastic dish on an orange crate next to his bedroll. It was like a holy man's room. This wasn't an alley in one of the world's most inhuman cities, it was a homey, comfy hobo jungle, a place where "nature's gentlemen" hang out. We'd often sit on milk cartons and drink brown bag wine, and one day we heated up some Vienna sausages on a little camp stove. The cats watched us from the avocado tree but they didn't dare come any closer.

This Roderick was a street intellectual. He was full of stories. When he was lushed up he'd tell the same tales again and again, but the details usually varied enough to keep it interesting. Roderick had a raffish charm and an innate sense of entitlement. He was perfectly at home in the street. You'd see him sitting on a park bench, telling stories to tourists or feeding the birds, somehow elegant in his crumpled tweed Borsalino hat and his tattered 43rd Infantry overcoat. Or else or you'd see him at a distance, strolling along Wilshire Boulevard, followed by a cloud of pigeons. Even though I'd just recently met him, Roderick for me in those days seemed already to be passing into myth, like Pecos Bill and Johnny Appleseed. He was a jongleur, a word juggler, a wandering minstrel who, in medieval times, would have been making the rounds of castles and abbeys and public marketplaces, entertaining the gentlefolk and commoners alike with his stories.

"In India," he told me one day, "there are Brahmin priests who chant sacred mantras that have been passed down from father to son for centuries. The mantras are in no known language. These sounds are thirty and forty thousand years old, passed down from generation to generation before the advent of human speech. They predate the birth of the spoken word. That's why they're holy."

Roderick had a heart. In fact he cried when the cat with the white paw got squashed by a car. He was really broken up about it, and so were skinny Leticia and Mad Rosa the Flower Lady. People thought Mad Rosa was crazy but what she had was a speech impediment. "Begonias?" she'd croak, "Begonias?" That was about all she could say. Those flowers of hers were pretty bedraggled. I think she stole them from graveyards. Mustafa didn't like Mad Rosa hanging around. He'd tell skinny Leticia: "What is this, a goddamn funeral?" It was bad for business, he said. But everyone adored Mad Rosa, and Roderick would buy her breakfast sometimes when he was bucks up. I don't think they were lovers but who knows. I will say that the two of them, Roderick and Mad Rosa, were fixtures in Lafayette Park, every bit as much as the pigeon-shit splooped statue of the Marquis de Lafayette or the whores in gauzy summer dresses who sprawled lazily on the grass bordering the sidewalk, offering their wares to passersby. If you were a tourist and you hadn't come to the park specifically to buy drugs or get laid, you could join Roderick and Mad Rosa on their park bench and Roderick would tell you a story and Mad Rosa would sell you a flower. Not a bad way to spend an afternoon in the City of the Angels.

"Death is nothing," Skylar is fond of saying with a twist of his fingers, as if he were crumbling a cracker in his soup. "Death is nothing. What is death, after all? A transition from one state to another. What could be more simple, more natural?"

I like Skylar, but I'm suspicious of people who say that death is nothing. I can't help wondering if they've ever really tried it.

Right after Halloween Skylar hired me to punch up his script and to help him develop a suitable stage name. I was busting suds part time at the China Doll on South Broadway—$8.25 an hour and all the subgum duck you can eat—so I was grateful for the gig. Skylar was getting ready for open mic night at the Fluffy Bunny. He makes the rounds of venues in LA, San Francisco and New York, appearing in drag and talking about forced feminization and his life as a cross dresser. Skylar has tons of money and can afford to indulge his every whim.

The work on the script went swimmingly and Skylar

invited me to lunch at his palatial home in Brentwood. Maybe I shouldn't have taken the liberty of inviting Pompeii Press editor Cliff English because Cliff had always been a difficult person and he and Skylar had never gotten along, going all the way back to the days when the three of us first met in Paris, but Cliff was a pal and there was a good chance that Skylar's Japanese chef would be serving Cliff's favorite mascarpone cheesecake.

We were sitting by the pool with our umbrella drinks.

"Today," Skylar began, "I'm wearing a lace underwire padded bra underneath my shirt."

"What's for lunch?" Cliff interrupted. Cliff was in a nasty mood and not at all inclined to listen to Skylar's shtick.

"Lunch? Vegetable samosas."

"Vegetable samosas! You mean we took the bus all the way to Brentwood for vegetable samosas? Skye, when I pronounce the word 'lunch' I am thinking of some plump, succulent creature that perhaps only moments ago was flitting through a sunlit forest uttering wild careless cries of joy."

"Jesus, Cliff," I muttered, giving him a good jolt in the ribs with my elbow. We were off to a bad start. I was properly horrified at Cliff's behavior, and Skylar was of course miffed, and I could tell he was pissed off at me too for including this arrogant little man in our lunch plans.

"Do you remember, Donald, why you went to Paris?"

I remember, Skye. I went to Paris to write a book. That's what you do when you're young, right? You go to Paris and write a book. It seems laughable now, looking back. A twenty-year-old boy? Write a book? Besides, there's so much more to do in Paris when you're young.

"Do you remember, Cliff," Skylar said, "how we sat in the Café de Flore and talked about the books we would one day write? The world-shattering books, the apocalyptic books?"

"The book I always wanted to write," Cliff intoned

dreamily. "Yeah, the Paris book. Sure, I remember. That's how I think of it now, after all these years. *The Paris book.* World-shattering? Apocalyptic? You better believe it! The Apocalypse on wheels is what I wanted my book to be. Jerk the rug out from under everybody, that was my idea. I honestly didn't know whether I wanted to write a book or build a 100-megaton bomb. I mean, we were young. You remember, Donald, how it was. Bring it down. Bring everything down. That was all I could think of in those days."

I thought Cliff was smoothing things over with this talk about the old days in Paris, but Skylar was still peeved, and he took his anger out on me. "I think it's scandalous the way Donald makes characters out of his friends," he snapped. "You're one of them, you know, Cliff. You realize what he's doing, don't you?"

"Like I give a rat's ass."

"How do you justify that, Donald? How can you justify making characters out of your friends?"

"I'm turning state's evidence, that's all. Besides, nobody's going to read it anyway."

"Why are you doing what you're doing, Skye?" Cliff countered. "Why appear on stage at the Fluffy Bunny in a Diane Von Furstenberg neon red dress and confess your innermost secrets and all that?"

"Simple, Cliff. For the same reason that you write books. It's necessary for the healing of my inner child."

"Your inner child is perfectly healthy, homes. It's the rest of your shit that's fucked up."

I thought the two of them were going to duke it out, but after several more drinks we waded bravely through the vegetable samosas and Kenji-san brought out the mascarpone cheesecake and everything was, in Skylar's words, "ticketyboo."

One Friday a few weeks later when things were slow at the China Doll Ping Chao gave me the afternoon off. I caught a bus up to Fairfax. Skye was pleased with my work on the script and had just presented me with a nice check. His birthday was coming up and I wanted to get him something special. After a stop at Canter's Deli for pastrami on rye, a beer and those glorious kosher pickles, I found a vintage clothing boutique.

"This is a Marilyn Monroe prom dress. The bodice is boned, you see, and these two chiffon scarves meet at the bust and flow down the back. These are handset pearls, incidentally. This dress is vintage all the way. It's a beautiful dress. Who's the lucky lady?"

"It's for a man."

Now we're seated, the three of us, Skylar, Cliff and me, on the terrace of the Café Royale at the Wilshire Royale Hotel. My old friend, Dante, the chef, brings the champagne and the glasses. He's making his special kallaloo. I went with Dante, in fact, the day before to Grand Central Market to get the pig's tails and fish heads he puts in the stew.

"Dat's me bredder," he says, clapping me on the back. "Hah, hah, hah! Dat's me bredder!"

"Donald, it was wonderful of you to give me this party," Skylar begins. "I appreciate it so much. You know, I simply adore the faded elegance of Wilshire Boulevard. There's this sense of the past, of Hollywood's Golden Era, combined now with an interesting overlay of tagging and graffiti, and it's all so very fertile and ugly-beautiful and ticketyboo."

Skylar gets out his bifocals and reads my card. "I'm not at all sure that birthdays are something to celebrate. After a certain age, I mean."

"Oh, shit, Skye, fifty-six isn't old. Go ahead, open your present."

"Oh my God, Donald! A pink prom dress!"

"It's a *Marilyn Monroe* pink prom dress."

"Wow, these twin chiffon scarves will really set off my boobies. Thanks, Donald! What do you think, Cliff?"

"Yeah, you tits'll look great in that dress. No question

about it."

By the time we'd finished our champagne and the kallaloo the setting sun's rays, slanting through a lens of smog, were filling the sky with crushed peach dust and igniting the copper roof of Bullock's Wilshire, which for me is *the* symbol of LA, like St. Patrick's in New York and the Eiffel Tower in Paris. Cliff and I were about to pack Skylar into a taxi, but instead he ordered more champagne. Skye was in a buoyant mood and he wanted to talk about the perfect stage name he was certain I was going to create for him.

"It's just amazing what press agents can do. A little twist is all it takes. Fortunately, you, Donald, have the same kind of mind. The *name, the name!* The name makes all the difference, the difference between being a star and being a nothing. It's the difference, for example, between Norma Jean Baker and Marilyn Monroe. Don't you agree? What would Archibald Leach's life have been like if he hadn't become Cary Grant? Or John Wayne if he hadn't been John Wayne? I mean, it's hard to imagine Marion Michael Morrison kicking ass on the Chisolm Trail. Sometimes it's just a little touch, that little touch of genius. That's why I've got you, Donald my boy. Jan Michael Vincent's original name was Michael Vincent, but when they added the 'Jan' it gave his persona a whole new European spin. Then there's that famous thing about Theda Bara. Theda Bara is an anagram for 'Arab Death.' Did you know that? Who would have thought you could make a woman's name out of Arab Death?"

And from here back around to the *Death is Nothing* theme, and then to the Norwegian salmon he's going to be serving at an upcoming dinner in Brentwood to which Cliff and I are not invited.

"Before the fish are slaughtered they're immersed in very cold water which has the effect of putting them into hibernation, thus preserving enzymes which would otherwise be lost. They're chilled to around 10 degrees centigrade while they're still alive. Then chilling doesn't cause the fish any distress because they're already naturally cold-blooded. I saw it—"

"We know," Cliff muttered. "You saw it on the Internet."

"I want to thank you both for being so open-minded. I always feel so much more comfortable when I'm wearing my boobs. So safe and so cherished and so ticketyboo! I'd like to thank you especially, Donald. I feel like I could tell you anything. But I also feel that your willingness to listen is predicated to some extent upon your need to make a character out of me. I can't help feeling too that you patronize me sometimes. You don't mind my saying that, do you? I know you think I'm a dilettante. But the truth is, I'm just like you, you and Cliff. We're three of a kind.

"You put your finger on it the other day at the pool, Donald, when you talked about turning state's evidence. It's the need to confess, to come out of the closet, to go public. The need to go public, that's what we share. Confession is good for the soul, isn't that right? It's healing. We haven't come here to *get* something; we've come here to give something to the world, even though the world may not give a shit. There's something we have to get off our chest. You might even say we have to get something *out of* our chest. It's a need to turn ourselves inside out, like the starfish. We've got to rip our guts out by the handful and scatter them to the four winds.

"The normal man is looking to get his battery charged. Our batteries are already charged and overcharged. We're sending out signals, like the radio signals astronomers send into deep space. *Anybody home?* We're hoping to find another being out there in the emptiness who will resonate with us. That's why we do what we do. It's a lonely business. I don't have to tell you that."

"Maybe we've been demagnetized."

"No, Cliff, it's the opposite. We're filled with magnetic particles but we're flying under their radar. Not because we want to. It's the way we're made. How to manifest oneself completely, that's the question. It's almost a matter of pixels per inch, in a way of speaking. We've got to make ourselves visible to them. I'm lucky because I'm a performance artist. They have to listen to me. Of course they can leave the theater...

"It's different with the printed word. It's not time for you yet, Donald, I'm sorry to say. Your readers are in the embryo. God, my tits are getting sweaty. Do you want some more champagne?"

Skylar waved his hand and Dante, ever attentive, brought another chilled bottle of bubbly, hot coffee and some crumbly squares of pistachio baklava.

"But coming back to the slaughter of the innocents. I mean, the slaughter of the salmon. Have you ever noticed that when you take the 's' off the word 'slaughter' it becomes 'laughter?' That's the way it is with the gods. They mow us down for kicks. They're laughing as we go through our machinations on this dear old surface. We're a dime a dozen to them. Kill us off in wholesale lots—nine million in World War I, fifty million in World War II—and we spring up like blades of grass, more and more of us. Sure, death is nothing, but each person is unique, just as every snowflake is unique. No two alike. I saw it on the Internet. We don't count and yet we do count. It's up to us.

"We—we three—we've got to make a statement, not just spawn and die. In my case, if I stay in the closet, I haven't manifested myself fully. It's a one-time trip, guys— one chance we have to express what has never been expressed before and will never be repeated. Norma Jean Baker is the given. That's what you're issued in the delivery room when the doctor slaps you on the ass and sends you spinning into the world. Marilyn Monroe is the *possibility,* the potential that lies in every one of us. Norma Jean is the caterpillar stage. Marilyn Monroe is the butterfly. Occasionally there's someone who skips the caterpillar stage altogether and just steps out of the cradle fully winged and fully armed. Mozart, for example. But most people settle for being Norma Jean Baker. They don't even know the Marilyn Monroe part of them exists. Or maybe they catch a faint glimpse of it sometimes when they're drunk or on acid, like a last-quarter moon fading on the horizon. Everybody is Norma Jean Baker, but only a few of us get to be Marilyn Monroe."

One night a week or so later at the China Doll, after I'd pulled the filters and stocked the line and wiped everything down and Ping Chao had checked and checked again and I was mopping the floor for what I hoped to God was the last time, I found myself thinking once more about the old days in Paris and about the book I always wanted to write. Not the books I'd written, not those books, but the real book, the Paris Book, the apocalyptic book you write in Paris when you're young and pure and brave. I didn't want to crank out another Plastic Christ with a removable pancreas for the laboratory specialists to dissect in their cold white morgues. I wanted a book that would bite, a book that could wound, a book with the power to maim. I wanted to write a book that would be a criminal act. I'd print the book myself if I had to, I'd chop down the trees to make the paper, I'd capture the squid and wring the ink from their pores with my own two hands.

The reflection of a red neon beer sign shimmered on the wet kitchen floor as I began rinsing out my mop. Ping Chao was marrying the condiments. I never wrote that Paris Book, my apocalyptic buzzbomb, but just the same the bomb went off. The bomb exploded but the words remain, words that snarl like shards of twisted metal, words that beckon like severed hands, words that toll like wedding bells clanging far out at sea. The halibut understands my words, the dire wolf understands me perfectly, the pelican understands, the narwhal understands. It's only my own kind with whom I can't communicate.

6

"Sol Fingerbein is so cheap he goes to an amateur dentist." This choice plum from Cliff English. I can't tell you why Cliff would talk this way about Sol Fingerbein, except to say that Cliff was bitter, bitter about a lot of things. We were at la Pachanga, where I sometimes met with Cliff to discuss my next Pompeii crotch novel. According to Cliff, this amateur dentist of Sol's has his war-surplus equipment set up in the parlor of a boarding house in the Fairfax district. The guy's a heavy juicer. Before he can operate, he has to be half in the bag.

"You sit in an easy chair and he goes at you with a jeweler's drill," Cliff told me, slopping some chipotle sauce on his carne asada burrito. "Interesting guy. He used to be a jeweler, a veterinarian and an embalming fluid salesman. Does a little taxidermy on the side."

I sometimes wish Cliff wouldn't speak so disparagingly about Sol Fingerbein. It was Sol Fingerbein, after all, who introduced me to Doreen, back in the Bareback Book days. Doreen was—or is—the Queen of the Angels. She worked at Queen of Angels Hospital, in fact, on Alvarado, just off the Hollywood Freeway, as a nurse's aide, until she was caught, one Christmas Eve, sucking off the night janitor on a morgue table. Doreen is the woman who posed for several of the cover illustrations Sol Fingerbein did for Bareback Books.

To get to the point, Doreen and I became friendly right away. One night at Sol's studio on Seventh, near the Orpheum Theater, Doreen and I got together in the shower. After the hot water was gone and we'd concluded our slippery pleasure, we rushed out to Mon Kee in Chinatown where we wolfed down huge platters of garlic squid, cashew chicken and shrimp-fried rice. Frantically, we made plans for the future. Doreen shared my passion for food and wine. We couldn't get enough, just as we couldn't get enough of each other.

After that night in Sol Fingerbein's shower, Doreen and I kept steady company. It was as if we'd been married for decades. She was living at the time in Hollywood. You could see the Capitol Records building from her bedroom window. Always when we'd get together at her place I managed to bring a bottle of wine, even if I had to borrow the money to buy it. Every weekend it was the same. I rang the bell, Doreen greeted me with a lingering kiss, I'd crack open the wine, Doreen would bring the glasses, we'd plop down on the couch, I'd pour, and we'd toast:

"To us!"

I don't mean to imply that ours was an exclusive relationship. It was far from that. I mean, from the beginning Doreen was throwing open her petals to other pollinators. Her agent, photographers, this director and that. I tried not to think about her infidelities, but she had a sneaky way of bringing the subject up. Invariably, the wine prompted Doreen to tell me about everything she'd been doing during the week, and invariably her doings boiled down to a series of encounters which she referred to as her "escapades." And unfailingly she described these escapades of hers in explicit detail.

"I have to tell you about my latest escapade. Flávio.

He's a soccer player—you know, *fútbol*. I met him at the
Bonaventure Hotel—the revolving cocktail lounge on the
34th floor. We came back here for a drink. We had some
wine in the Jacuzzi. What a body! He's built like a Greek
god. He wanted me to go down on him so I did. I sucked
his cock. He came in my mouth. Then we fucked. God, it
was incredible. In the Jacuzzi, on the couch, in the hallway,
on the kitchen table. Baby, I'll tell you this, he's the most
virile man I've ever met. And what a cock! I couldn't begin
to get it all into my mouth. He fucked me for hours. Good
Christ, Baby, he's an animal! I thought he'd split me in half.
I sat down on him and he twirled me around like a top. I
was helpless in his hands. And such big hands, too. So
strong, so masculine. His chest! And his shoulders. God,
he's built like an oak. He kept zinging in on my clit and I
got off and off. It was wonderful. When he finally came he
pulled his big beautiful cock out of my pussy and squirted
his hot cum all over my tits. It was the most erotic thing
I've ever seen. I rubbed his cum into my nipples. That got
him excited all over again and of course we ended up in
bed. I actually fell asleep with his cock in my mouth..."

In all fairness, I think part of the reason Doreen felt
she had to tell me everything was because at the time I was
writing her autobiography, "The Oomph Girl." Her title,
not mine. Doreen loved the movies, especially the old
movies, so we went often to the New Beverly Cinema
where we saw "Angels with Dirty Faces" with James
Cagney three nights in a row. Cagney's costar was the
beautiful Ann Sheridan, whose Hollywood soubriquet was
"the Oomph Girl," and Doreen who, by her own
admission—and mine—bore a striking resemblance to
Ann Sheridan, appropriated the title for herself and
incorporated it in her portfolio and on her business cards.
Often in the evenings after a vigorous tussle, as we were
lying side by side on her bed gazing up at the sparkly
plastic angels dangling from the bedroom ceiling, Doreen
would murmur, "Baby, about the book. You can talk about

my escapades all you want. I think the readers deserve that. But listen, please don't tell them that I'm not a natural blonde, okay?"

"No worries, Kid. Your secret is safe with me."

Right after I got started with Doreen I moved from my dismal digs at the Rosslyn to mid-Wilshire, the Wilshire Royale Hotel at 2619 Wilshire Boulevard, a cozy room with air conditioning, steam heat, Old World plumbing and a panoramic view of Hollywood, including the famous Hollywood sign, the white dome of the Griffith Park Observatory and the old Queen of Angels Hospital—now abandoned, a movie set—where Doreen—the "Oomph Girl"—once worked. It was the heyday of the Bareback Books period and I was doing okay financially.

Cold nights in the room... The heat came on automatically. So reassuring, the radiator hissing, steam heat, it was delightful. And the bath with its *ancien fitments*, my Old World plumbing. On Thursday, my maid's day, after breakfast downstairs at the Café Royale, I'd go back up to the room, throw open the door, and what a miracle. I never tired of that moment, the bed changed, the room sparkling clean, wrapped plastic glasses on the dresser, my personal effects rearranged, the fresh towels, and the fragrant hotel soap heaped on the bathroom sink.

Dante, the hotel chef, used to read the Bible every morning. "That is my food," he'd tell me. Thank God he allowed me something more substantial. Mornings I'd type on the hotel patio. After I'd seated myself Dante would emerge from the back door of the Café Royale, perennial hangout of the Rampart Precinct vice cops, with coffee and often with orange juice, toast, bacon and eggs, all gratis, courtesy of Chef Dante. He wouldn't let me pay for anything. After all, I was a writer, and writers are special people. Later on, he might bring me a bowl of the Jamaican clam chowder he was preparing for lunch. Dante always insisted that his Jamaican clam chowder was homemade. Me, I think he just added a few random ingredients to the canned stuff. But that's neither here nor there. This was a Man, Dante, and he cared about writers, a very rare thing.

Dante came from St. Thomas. He had seven children. He prayed every day at St. Basil's, just up the street on Wilshire. Carried a 38 Special in a holster. A real guy, Dante. Played the piano, too. Always bucks up. Who knows where he got his money. It wasn't from cooking. He was forever asking if he could do anything for me. A small loan perhaps? He'd peel a few crisp bills off his roll. Fine, if not now, would I please let him know if there's anything, anything at all. He, Dante, understood how it is with writers.

Afternoons I'd go by the Cafe Royale. The busboy would be hurrying with dishes, the cops would be just leaving. Dante would break out the beers. Again I couldn't pay. Nothing was too good for me. "My friend," Dante would say with a huge grin, his mustache breaking away from his big white teeth, "you are a writer..."

And the Wilshire Royale was a writers' hotel, make no mistake about that. It was a hotel for writers who don't write. You'd hear them in the bar talking out their books to anyone who'd listen, and in the elevator, talking options, rewrites, back-end deals. Everyone supposedly had a script, a contract, an agent.

It was good, though, living at mid-Wilshire, and good too to have money in my pocket. Doreen and I went often to the Vagabond Theater—*the* place for old movies—around the corner from the Park Plaza Hotel. We *saw Lost Horizon, Arsenic and Old Lace, It Happened One Night, The Great Caruso, Showboat, Gone With The Wind, Babes on Broadway, Bus Stop, White Christmas, The Maltese Falcon* and *It's a Wonderful Life*, with James Stewart and Donna Reed.

The theater was cozy and dark, a great place to mush it up, and Doreen always had her hand in my pants. One night she made me squirt in the middle of *Mister Deeds Goes to Town*. That got her so hot we locked ourselves in the ladies' room and pulled off a quick one with her squatting on the toilet seat and me standing over her like a rapist.

It's a Wonderful Life!

After the movie we'd go to Mi Guatemala on Hoover, or Langer's Deli, or, if we were in the mood for Flip food, the Jeepney Grill on Alexandria for bulalo soup or oxtail pochero, or even, in a pinch, the immortal Tommy's, corner of Beverly and Rampart, for the chili cheeseburger and fries. Or we'd head for Chinatown, Pho 79, my favorite Vietnamese soup restaurant. A huge bowl of broth—pho—tasting of garlic and cinnamon, loaded with noodles, cilantro, green onions and thin slices of rare beef. With it a plate of raw bean sprouts, Vietnamese basil, sliced chili peppers and lemon quarters. You shovel the bean sprouts into the soup with your chopsticks and fish out the noodles.

During this period I was nuts about Chinatown. I loved the mysterious faces and the intriguing glances and the parasols the women carry, and the food shops, crabs and lobsters and fish swimming alive in tanks, waiting to be snatched out and gobbled up, glazed ducks, and the roasted pigs dangling from hooks, fragrant, delicious, golden brown, with crispy ears and blissful porcine smiles.

A golden period. I was happy. Bareback Books consumed most of my energies and the Oomph Girl did the rest.

A golden period, yes, but the seeds of my destruction were already blowing in the wind. I knew that Doreen was seeing other men. I tried not to think about it. There was one guy in particular, Harvey, a used car salesman who lived in Bellflower.   My first meeting with Harvey took place at Ruby Fine's lawn party in Westwood. I didn't want to go to the party, but I knew I had to make an appearance and I couldn't let Doreen down, so I cut off my ponytail and allowed Doreen to buy me a pair of designer jeans and an expensive Tommy Bahama silk shirt. Everybody would be there, everybody meaning the

Bareback Books crew—Fausto, Norma Jacoby, Cliff English, Sol Fingerbein and Wally Featheringill, the retired Marine colonel from Cardiff-by-the-Sea. And of course Ruby Fine and her angelic contingent of tough homosexual dreadnoughts. But most importantly for Doreen, our Bareback Books cover girl, some Hollywood producer types from Pacific Palisades would be in attendance, or so Norma Jacoby had promised. Doreen had arranged for Harvey to meet us later, she informed me as I scrubbed her back in the shower, but the Oomph Girl needed to be wearing a fellow on her arm when she made her grand entrance at the soiree. So the shmooze was on, and I was elected.

It was late afternoon when we arrived at the party. We'd polished off several bottles of white zinfandel with lunch and we were already quite drunk. Doreen was in an ebullient mood. The wine had engendered in her a fierce world-embracing optimism, and when she quickly spotted a couple of producer types—bald heads, cigars—she was certain in her heart of hearts that her big break was just a hand job away.

Ruby's lawn, easily the size of a "*fútbol*" field, was manicured like a golf green. An ersatz marimba band was stationed in a beribboned gazebo, and around a circular pool bordered by flowers and globe lights women wearing elbow-length gloves, floppy hats, strings of pearls and sporting long cigarette holders clutched tiny fluffy dogs and danced with men from West Hollywood in pastel three-piece seersucker suits. Ruby had even imported some supposedly colorful characters from Venice Beach—a guy with a parrot on his shoulder, a woman with an iguana, a dwarf riding a unicycle, etc. A squawking peacock wandered over the green expanse of lawn, posturing and preening, hardly distinguishable from the strolling guests.

Strangely enough Ruby Fine herself was nowhere in sight. Norma informed me confidentially that Ruby liked to survey the goings on from a distance, like the Great

Gatsby, perched on the verandah of her palatial home with a pair of binoculars. Not that I was anxious to see her. You have to understand, an encounter with Ruby Fine can be devastating. She'll pull you in with a toothy smile and a lot of gobbledygook about the female orgasm and before you know what's happening she extrudes her stomach and liquefies your flesh with powerful digestive juices, leaving nothing more than a bundle of bones.

As dusk began to fall the fur boas came out, and the balloons and the paper streamers, and around the pool the globe lights took on a soft amber glow while footmen in bow ties carved huge fragrant rounds of roast beef. The dancers, emboldened by the alcohol and the gathering darkness, switched from the twist to the tango, their ferocious gyrations punctuated by the incessant popping of champagne corks as toast after toast heaped praise upon our curiously absent hostess. The occasion for the party? The publication of Ruby Fine's latest Lila Nero classic, *Kiss My Clit*.

While Doreen was trawling the party for producer types I had a confab with Norma Jacoby. Norma was very chummy. "Ruby's been asking about you, Donaldo," she chirped as she dipped a carrot stick in some sort of whitish goop that looked suspiciously like pigeon shit. "She wants to have lunch next week."

"I'd sooner have lunch with Idi Amin."

I made a beeline for the caviar but was intercepted by Doreen. She'd snagged a runty Italian film director named Gianni Crimini. There was something sinister and not quite real about this Crimini. He was flanked by two torpedoes who looked like they'd stepped off the set of Goodfellas, and he supposedly drove a replica of James Dean's 1955 Porsche Spyder. The guy had the bling all right but I doubted like hell that this self-important little prick was actually a film director and a "kingpin of the new spaghetti western renaissance," as Doreen excitedly blurted when I shook his hand. As soon as I could I slipped out of their clutches and stuffed myself with roast beef, lox and caviar. At least the eats were decent. "Let's bounce," I told Doreen, but no, she already had her hand in Gianni's fly. Then one of the Venice Beach types asked me to dance and I lost track of Doreen—we were both spifficated— and sometime later I saw her sitting in the pool, her dress soaking wet. I couldn't tell if she was crying or not, but things had gone badly, I gathered, with Gianni. He was standing in the drive next to the Porsche—the Porsche was real—shouting in Italian at one of the elbow-length opera glove ladies. I understood some of it. He was telling the woman that her fluffy little dog couldn't go with them because it might piss in the car.

Suddenly one of the bodyguards stepped forward and began strangling the pooch and the woman let out a horrified screech. I thought that thug was going to throttle the life out of that little dog but Gianni called him off— "*Basta! Basta!*"—and Gianni and the woman and the dog piled into the Porsche and peeled out in a great shower of gravel and sparks, and Salvatore and Guido followed in a sleek black limo.

Doreen, dripping wet, went to powder her nose and Norma introduced me to the Colonel. I'd never met Colonel Featheringill before, but he was, predictably, an odd duck. He cornered me by the punchbowl, balancing his champagne goblet, jabbing with a smoldering cigar. He wanted to know all about my "process." It was plain to see that the man actually considered himself a literary figure.

"How do you...go about it, I mean, the writing?"

"Actually, I don't write. I masturbate into the typewriter."

I was hugely relieved when Harvey finally showed up and he and Doreen whisked me away from the Colonel.

Harvey was well past fifty, narrow in the chest, potbellied, dyspeptic, and he smoked long stiletto-like cigars, Garcia y Vega panatelas. On top of this he had bushy eyebrows that were continually shedding a snowstorm of dandruff flakes on his reading glasses, and worse, on his mustache. He was, in other words, a most unlikely candidate for Doreen's hand.

Doreen, in her seemingly innocent way, had often blabbed about their sex life. His prick, she informed me one day over chili-cheeseburgers at Tommy's, was rather too thin for her liking.

"It feels," she murmured, "exactly like he's fucking me with one of those damned cigars."

I'd never thought of Harvey as much of a threat, but I guess I should have gotten the message when, several weeks after Ruby's party, he and Doreen flew to Catalina for lunch. The next thing I knew they were island hopping. Maui, Molokai, Oahu. I heard through the grapevine that Harvey had left his wife. Pulled his savings out of the bank, too. They'd kept on going, I learned, the lovebirds. Papeete, Pago Pago, Bora Bora. Doreen was in a great mood. Postcards were pinging off me like tracer bullets. Then silence, a long silence. Then a postcard from Paris, the Hotel Sofitel. "The Champs Elysée is glorious this time of year..."

Well, of course it is, goddamn it!

Doreen, Queen of the Angels, the Oomph Girl. She left me to wander the streets of LA like a broken toy. I imagine she's married by now. Getting fat, eating *paté de foie*. Not married to Harvey, I don't mean that. She probably dumped Harvey right after Paris. In fact I heard that Harvey was back at the used car lot in Bellflower. And Doreen? Barcelona, most likely. She'd often talked about Barcelona. She was over the moon about Barcelona, I remember. No shortage of *fútbol* players in Barcelona. Plenty of bullfighters too, I imagine. She'd have her choice of pricks. Matadors, picadors, banderilleros... Well, the hell with it.

7

It's the beginning of my third month at this huge old house on Highland, and I think I've found a home. The kitchen is my domain; I do the cooking, wrestle with the pots and pans, etc. Every morning I cook breakfast for Big Edna, who owns the place. We can see the Hollywood Sign from the front window, important, at least to Big Edna, because she has a thing about the Hollywood Sign. She's obsessed with Peg Entwistle, the beautiful British actress who committed suicide in 1931 by jumping off the top the Hollywood Sign's 50-foot tall letter "H." She keeps a list of recent Hollywood suicides too, gorgeous moths who fluttered too close to La La Land's mesmerizing flame. This probably means that she's harboring a death wish, meaning she'd like to off herself, something like that, or at least she likes to imagine that she would.

It's tragic what life does to beautiful girls. Not just the ones like Peg Entwistle who commit suicide, I don't mean that. I'm talking about the passage of time, what it does to you. Take Big Edna, for instance. Big Edna was beautiful once. Now she looks like the Piltdown Man. How do I know Big Edna was beautiful? There's a photo of her in the dining room, a family portrait featuring her mother and father and three sisters perched demurely on a sofa, obviously America, circa 1950's. Interesting, because people back then were still halfway human, and the young girls with their dreamy, creamy expressions are smiling in a sickly half disbelieving way as if they'd just gotten a sudden glimpse of the sorry fucking circus into which they were about to be launched like svelte kissy-wet torpedoes.

Fortunately Big Edna has the sop of religion. "Give your pain to the Baby Jesus!" That's what I hear her telling her son Joffker all the time. "Give your pain to the Baby Jesus!" As if the Baby Jesus didn't already have enough pain. The Baby Jesus is sorted for pain. That's my conviction.

It all started with a call from Starz, I mean my tenure at the big old house on Highland. He was back in town, undergoing shock treatments at the Veterans Hospital, I learned. Good old Starz! It had been how long since Malibu? Of course I decided to drop by the hospital and look in on him.

I was surprised when Starz met me in the hospital lobby. He was wearing his old Paris-days Che Guevara t-shirt, which usually meant he'd probably get us into trouble with the law or worse. "I'm out of this motherfucker," he muttered savagely. He was serious. He was booking, leaving *tout de suite*, going AMA. I tried to talk him out of it, but he was determined.

"Fucking world!" he snarled. He'd been fired from a job in Ohio and had picked up a hefty severance check but the state slapped a lien on it. Then he got evicted and began living in his car. "It was the same day my kids called me from Disneyland," he muttered, biting frantically at his lips. "I'm getting too old for this shit, man." He seemed close to tears, but a split second later he was all smiles. It was eerie, I can tell you. Standing there in the hospital lobby he flung his hands wide and bowed like a master of ceremonies, then beamed delightedly at me and flashed a tricky wink. "But I have to say it makes a great scene for a film," he blurted. "Don't you think? The homeless father talking on the phone to his kids? While they're at fucking Disneyland? Eating ice cream cones and shit? It's enough to make a cop cry!"

Outside on the steps he confided that he was sorry to be leaving a girl he'd just met at the hospital. "I keep meeting these really great girls in insane asylums," he said. "We're like ships that pass in the night." And the doctors: "The doctors here are full of shit. They keep telling me that I've got to adapt to reality. But why should I adapt to reality when what I want is a different reality?"

We went to Maria's at Grand Central Market for the fish tacos and after we'd downed a few beers everything seemed almost like it was in the Malibu days, back when Starz and I were living at the beach house.

"Hey, it's good to see you, man," Starz said suddenly. It was as if he'd just noticed that I was there, sitting across the table from him. He seized my hand and squeezed it so hard that I almost let out a yelp. "I've got a movie in me, homes, I know I have," he said, rolling his eyes back in his head and sweating great drops of sweat. "I couldn't do it back there, man. Not in tight-ass Ohio. I just couldn't. I mean how can you blossom when you can't even fucking breathe?"

There was a girl named Tiffany in the picture, Starz informed me hastily as his cell phone tweetled. "She's here," he announced. We hurriedly polished off our beers and stepped over to the fish counter where a strange haunted girl was lurking behind a pile of goggle-eyed squid. "You swear they're watching you," she muttered with a thin nervous laugh as I shook her hand.

We got on a bus. Tiffany had recently busted out of the women's prison in Chowchilla, I learned. She'd slept under bridges and had stolen sun-warmed tomatoes from farmers' fields before making safe haven at her grandmother's house on Highland.

"You don't remember anything." Starz was talking now about how it felt to get the juice. "They wheel me in, the guy puts the thing over my face. I breathe a couple of times and I'm gone. This last time when I woke up the craziest phrases were going through my mind. Stuff like...*and they basted the bacons of the Foxes of Harrow with fistfuls of blancmange.* Now where did I get that, do you know? Rabelais? Chaucer maybe? *Finnegan's Wake?*"

"You'll be fine, Honeybun," Tiffany murmured inanely.

"I've got a movie in me, man," Starz muttered desperately a moment later as I gawked from the bus window at a mysterious hijab woman standing in front of the Sumito Bank building. He kept repeating the phrase over and over, and Tiffany kept nodding her head resolutely and murmuring in a patronizing tone, "Of course you have, Honeybun." Passengers were glaring at us and a pretty lady and a rosy-cheeked little girl sitting across the aisle jumped up and changed their seats. I thought Starz and I were going to talk some more about a script or what have you, but when we arrived at the big old house on Highland Starz and Tiffany immediately rushed up to their room. "We'll talk tomorrow," Starz called to me from the stairs. It was too late now to head back home so I crashed on the couch.

The next day I met Tiffany's uncle Joffker and Olaf the handyman, then Starz and Tiffany and I spent the rest of the morning by the pool, sopping up coffee and Kahlua. Although Starz was technically homeless he seemed to be pretty well heeled. We ordered pepperoni pizzas with Kalamata olives and meatball sandwiches and drank German beer, and that night I cooked dinner for the lot, beef burgundy and Yorkshire pudding.

"Life is beautiful," Starz proclaimed joyfully, as he cracked open a bottle of Grand Mariner. Maybe the shock treatments had done him some good, I reflected. I didn't say anything about a script or ask him what he had in mind. I figured I'd give him some room to breathe, get settled in, and all that. He definitely seemed much more together now than he had at Maria's and on the bus ride. Maybe it was the shock treatments or it could have been a good night's sleep that did it, or maybe it was having Tiffany by his side. Hard to believe, strange creature that she was, but who can say when it comes to what the world calls love? In any case the transformation was complete. He was back to being the old Starz now, the Malibu Starz.

December 4th or 5th. Several weeks have passed and I'm at a loss as to where to pick up the thread. Brunsvigga is here with us now, one of the androgynous doyennes of the night, a hulking lesbian with muscles of steel and a shrill piercing whinny that's guaranteed to set your teeth on edge. Brunsvigga is Joffker's keeper, his aide de camp, his nursemaid. Joffker? Joffker is a blob of undifferentiated protoplasm hooked up to a fierce mental dynamo. He spends his days wrestling with his pain. He's peering at me from his couch as I write this on a yellow pad, his head a dream machine cranked by a dyslectic monkey, his gaze the fishy stare of a guppy drowning in amniotic fluid. Now he's swimming toward me, his face blurred by a lens of water. Some portion of Joffker is still alive—the ravening maw, the distended stomach. All else the cancer of the mind has co-opted. Did you know, Joffker, that "pain" is "bread" in French? Bread and pain, both ubiquitous, you see. Give us this day our daily pain. *Le pain de campagne, le pain maudit, le pain perdu...*

When Brunsvigga first arrived from Reykjavik I thought she was Big Edna's psychotherapist, but it turns out she's a colonic irrigation specialist. She gives Big Edna a high enema every night and I cook her breakfast in the morning. That way we've got both ends covered.

Brunsvigga is Joffker's boiler tender. It's she who stokes the furnace, the fiery furnace of Joffker's suffering, with shovel after shovelful of coal as he goes down and down into the bituminous blackness of his despair. And now the place is full of coal dust and we're all sneezing away like a bunch of diseased rats. We've got black lung disease, the lot of us, not surprising because these days the whole fucking world is diseased, because this is the 21st century and the shell of the World Egg is cracking and the albumen is pouring out the windows faster than the bastards can shovel it back in. Poor Humpty Dumpty! It was a beautiful world, wasn't it, I mean once upon a time? You could drink the water, you could breathe the air. But now the question is, can Humpty Dumpty be put back together again? Answer: I doubt it like hell.

We've got rats too, real ones, or at least Big Edna says we do. She claims she can't sleep because she hears them inside the walls at night, creeping, chewing, squeaking, smacking their lips and pissing everywhere. She sees their tiny feverish eyes, their twinkling noses, their twitching whiskers, as she tosses and turns, her mind a maggot heap of crawling thoughts. She's awake half the night, poor thing, praying to the Baby Jesus. Big Edna sleeps with Joffker's umbilical cord under her pillow. She cherishes his fetal lifeline as one might cherish the decaying relic of a saint, but all this mumbo-jumbo hasn't helped much with the rats, so she keeps Olaf busy setting out traps. "Olaf, be sure and put more traps behind the fridge," she'll say, wringing her hands. "There's a nest back there, I'm sure of it." Big Edna's hands are a sight to behold, the fingers and thumbs pitted and raw, the nails splintered from cracking pistachio nuts. Big Edna is addicted to pistachio nuts. Not surprising because pistachio nuts are extremely addictive. I'm becoming addicted to pistachio nuts myself, in fact. But that's neither here nor there.

Olaf's our rat-catcher, by the way. He's been elected. Olaf's our in-house Pied Piper. "Yahh, yahh," he murmurs, patting his big belly. "Don't worry, Missus. I fix." Later, after he empties the garbage and tightens up the doofilckus on the gas stove. There's plenty of time, plenty of time for everything. "Yahh, yahh," he intones. Every time I hear that raspy mellow *yahh, yahh* of Olaf's, his voice seems to echo over the rooftops of the world, it embraces and informs the entire sentient universe. It's a voice from a bygone age, a voice from a lost age of innocence; it's the glad cry of a chanticleer proclaiming, in spite of everything, that all's right with the world.

Olaf is what is called a good soul. Unlike Joffker and Brunsvigga and Big Edna, his mind's not on a rampage. Instead, his head is filled with the nuts and bolts of life. *Practicality.* "Yahh, yahh," he mutters, his mild blue eyes twinkling behind his rimless glasses as he makes his rounds, pruning the shrubs, fixing a faucet, bathing the leaves of the rubber plant with milk, his shaggy mane of white hair tucked into a tattered tweed workman's cap cocked at a jaunty angle. Olaf, as far as I'm concerned, is the only healthy inmate of this godforsaken lunatic asylum. The man is none too bright and he's immeasurably better off for it, if you want my opinion. As long as he can fill his belly and empty his bowels, what's to worry? No angst and no Weltschmerz for this man. "Yahh, yahh," he says, patting his big belly. It's an entity in its own right, Olaf's belly. It intrigues me the way Olaf plods along with a solemn shuffling gait as if he were wheeling that enormous belly of his in a wheelbarrow. If you ever saw him coming at you, you'd want to salute that belly, trust me, same as you'd salute a fucking bird colonel or a five-star general.

Meanwhile the rats are busy behind the fridge, gnawing, squirming, squeezing out little black turds, their "Kalamata olives," and Joffker is swimming in amniotic fluid and Big Edna is cracking pistachio nuts and Brunsvigga is chronicling it all in her autobiography, "The Story of MY PAIN," which she's writing on a roll of bloody white butcher paper with a felt-tip pen. From time to time she wets the point of her pen by sticking the pen up her ass. "God, that feels good," she whimpers. "If only it weren't for this fucking coal dust..."

Olaf steps briskly to the fridge, cracks open a beer and

sucks it down in a single gulp. "Aahhh!" he exclaims. He mops the beer foam off his walrus mustache with his shirtsleeve, smiling contentedly as he rummages in the pocket of his coveralls for a screwdriver, then he lets out a tremendous belch. *Aahhh* again. Life is good. He hums to himself, a little ditty, then bursts into song, "*Im Himmel gibt's kein Bier, drum trinken wire es hier...*"

*L*ater. Joffker and Brunsvigga are arguing so I've moved my yellow pad into the bathroom in order to take advantage of the peace and quiet. It never fails: Big Edna goes out for pistachio nuts and the rest of these dizzy bastards get up to their tricks. But fortunately the bathtub faucet leaks, and there's something wonderfully refreshing and restorative, I find, about the musical gurgle of flowing water. The bathroom walls are plastered with cautionary signs penned by Big Edna: "Turn hot water OFF, Flush toilet FOUR TIMES, three short, one long," etc. This is how people communicate in the 21st century. They scribble notes in Morse Code to each other on shithouse walls. Three short and one long. It's the American way. One if by land and two if by sea.

I never intended to move into this huge old house on Highland in the first place. The whole thing, as I mentioned, was Starz's idea, Starz and Tiffany, but I rode in on Starz's coattails and one day flowed into another and things happened and I stayed on. Pretty soon Bernie, a retired jockey, joined us. Bernie was the quiet sort, spent most of his time in his room with a needle and a spoon. Next door to Bernie lived a man with Parkinson's disease who roamed the halls at night holding his fluttering hands in front of him as if they were on display. Street girls came and went, and "Zelda," older, obviously insane, wore tiny tight short skirts and thought the rest of us were stalking her. She'd crouch, reach in her purse and snap your photo. Then Tiffany and Starz vanished. You never knew with Starz. Here he comes, there he goes. Starz was never the sort of person who stays in one place for long.

After that things were quiet for a while. I'd mostly sit by the pool playing checkers with the jockey and mooning over Doreen. I tried not to think about Doreen but one day I saw two gossamer-winged damselflies hovering above the pool in a close abdominal embrace and that reminded me of Doreen. Everything reminded me of Doreen. I was sinking into a blue funk. Then Vanessa showed up, Vanessa from Azuza. Vanessa from Azusa was going to teach me about opera. "You *so* need to add opera to your portfolio," she counseled. There'd been a rash of proletariat heroes in the movies lately who were opera buffs, she explained. I'm not saying I was in love with Vanessa from Azusa. Besides, Vanessa wasn't around long. Vanessa from Azusa moved out right after the Colombians showed up. I remember because it was just a few days before the jockey died. The Colombians were a handful, believe me. They'd creep into the kitchen in the dead of night. I'd make something communal like spaghetti or lasagna and they were on it like piranhas.

Then the Cambodians arrived, and one thing and another happened and Brunsvigga pitched a hissy fit. Claimed that one of the Cambodians had stolen her gym bag containing her steroids and syringes, her passport and a 14-inch jellyrubber strap-on manufactured in Mogadishu. Of course the Cambodians said it was the Colombians that did it and the Colombians the Cambodians and so on.

A couple nights ago a savage earthquake jolted me right out of bed. Three point five on the Richter Scale, Brunsvigga said. Brunsvigga prides herself on reading the newspapers. She thinks that makes her a normal person. There've been tremors recently all along the San Andreas Fault, she says. I don't doubt it. The Earth is getting ready to shrug off the obscene fungus of civilization. And yesterday morning another jolt that nearly shook the house off its foundations. I thought it was the Big One, I figured sure enough Los Angeles is sinking into the Pacific Ocean like the lost continent of Atlantis, but it turned out that Brunsvigga dropped an Olympic bar and it went halfway through the kitchen floor.

*T*hursday or Friday. Several days have passed and Olaf has done a number on the rats. He put the zap on them. Poison. He's been roaming the house with his pitchfork all morning spearing rat carcasses behind the fridge, behind the stove, etc. Now it's afternoon and the rest of us are sitting around the kitchen table munching bread and swilling wine, and Brunsvigga's segmented torso is gleaming with sweat and her coconut-size deltoids are bulging with branching blue veins. She's been doing lateral raises with 60-pound dumbbells in between sets of heavy hack squats. Our bread, baked in thermodynamic ovens, basted with benzotrichloride and dimethyl aminoazobenzene, is buttered with coal dust and rat poison. *Le pain perdu*, if you will. But no one seems to mind, as long as there's plenty of wine to wash it down.

And there's more good news. The flies have arrived, Olaf informs us with a jovial grin, poking his shaggy head in the kitchen door. They're buzzing everywhere. A good sign because it means there are more dead rats, more rat carcasses rotting inside the walls. Soon our nostrils will be filled with the sweet sickish smell of decaying rat husks along with sulphur and brimstone and we'll dance a merry maggot dance while Olaf jabs at us with his devil's pitchfork. But everything's ducky, really. There's a big hole in the kitchen floor and we're sinking into the Pacific Ocean and our bread is buttered with benzotrichloride and we're out of pistachio nuts, but I'm over Doreen and we can see the Hollywood Sign from our window. And the Baby Jesus is here with us. Did I mention that? And I'm writing it all down on a yellow pad or on the shithouse wall, whichever you like. It comes to the same thing. In Morse Code, I should have added. One if by land and two if by sea...

8

April found me back in the old neighborhood, a stone's throw from the Wilshire Royale, sharing a gloomy garage apartment with Schvedchikov, a Russian sculptor I met at La Pachanga. My room was sparsely furnished—a lopsided bunk, a wobbly table and a rickety chair. Brittle brown cheesecloth curtains framed a single window that looked out on "Fellatio Alley," a dismal grotto where the crack whores of Lafayette Park serviced their customers.

Schvedchikov was an odd duck. He'd spent some time at the nuthouse up at Patton. He had a cat, a stray he'd adopted. An orange tabby, she'd scratch and even savagely bite, all the while grinning from ear to ear and purring contentedly. Schvedchikov said it probably went back to her childhood. He told me about a Russian lad he used to tutor who played rough with a kitten. "When the creature grew up she would jump up on you and draw blood. All in fun, you understand, just by way of saying hello. She simply thought that was the way one played."

I guess Doreen subscribed to that theory. She thought that was the way the game was played. And she's off to Barbados or wherever it was. She fucking drew blood, all right. But fuck that. I'm not going to get into it.

This Schvedchikov was an urban recluse. Claustrophobic was the word for our crib. The clutter was incredible, as if you'd blown into the place on the back of a cyclone. You had to step over piled-up boxes of old magazines to get to the kitchen, which was crammed with helium tanks, welding torches and bags of cement splitting open and spilling out, and the pantry was full of picks and shovels, as if we were going to dig for gold. "I used to be a sculptor," Schvedchikov told me, as if that somehow explained the disarray. But that didn't hit me right either. If you're a sculptor you're always a sculptor, aren't you? There's no such thing as "used to be" a sculptor. Besides, he showed me some photos of his work, anguished bronze studies of the crucified Christ that reminded me of the tortured etchings of Albrecht Dürer and Matthias Grünewald. No "recreational crucifixion" chez Monsieur Schvedchikov! No sir. A serious man, somber, resolute, and somehow reminiscent of Wagner, whose famous photo with the floppy black beret he had taped to the refrigerator. I mean the stubborn chin, the pugnacious look in his eye, an obstinate look, the look of a man with lofty ambitions, a man who's full of himself. And day and night he was playing *The Ride of the Valkyries*, Wilhelm Furtwängler conducting the Vienna Philharmonic Orchestra. Schvedchikov's head was teeming with Michelangelo figures engaged in titanic struggles, you could see it by the crazy glint in his eye as he trudged from room to room, puttering absent-mindedly with old radios he'd found in goodwill stores or plucked out of dumpsters, cocking a half attentive ear to cheerful inane disk jockeys whose tinny patter cruelly mimicked the sultry, full...throated voice of the muse who had undoubtedly once purred in his ear. Something had gone terribly wrong in this man's life, in his artistic life. It was as if that ferocious orange tabby cat was the world and the world had raked his guts out with steel claws. Or maybe the world itself had gone wrong, had gone haywire, which of course is the case, because today Wagner's Twilight of the Gods has descended on steel wheels and the Valkyries are selling their ass on Santa Monica Boulevard. Not only the great God Thor is dead, but the whole pantheon has gone down into the abyss.

As messy as he was, Schvedchikov did have one fastidious habit. From time to time he'd mop the bathroom floor with some sort of powerful disinfectant that made the whole place smell like a Mexican whorehouse at three in the morning. I never tried to clean up the apartment myself because Schvedchikov had his rabbit runs set up between the piles of junk and I didn't want to disturb anything. Schvedchikov wasn't the sort of man you'd want to piss off. Because I couldn't afford to eat in restaurants I went ahead and emptied out the fridge, which was packed full of junk like old radio tubes, soldering irons, roller skate wheels, rusty nails, balls of string and twisted skeins of wire. Then I plugged the fridge back in, and voila, it worked, although it did make an ominous ticking sound, as though a weighted pendulum were swinging back and forth inside it, *tick tock, tick tock!* Then I established my own rabbit runs, starting with a tunnel from my bedroom to the toilet and another one leading to the kitchen. Eventually I expanded my system of tunnels to the point where Schvedchikov and I never saw each other for days even though we both spent a lot of time in the apartment, because Schvedchikov's tunnels were mostly separate from mine. We'd creep through the maze like miners with lanterns on our hats, or like rats burrowing in a great wheel of cheese, without ever encountering one another in the labyrinth of junk.

Just the same it got to the point where I began to be afraid of Schvedchikov when a week or more would go by and I hadn't seen him and yet I knew he was lurking somewhere in the bowels of the labyrinth like the Minotaur, because I'd smell the disinfectant. At these moments, I'd pause in mid-tunnel, listening intently, and I'd whisper distractedly to myself, "My God, what do you suppose he's cooking up? After all, he is a lunatic." *And don't terrorists sometimes make bombs out of old radio parts?* I began to have the craziest thoughts. Like maybe that tick-tocking refrigerator was actually a time bomb and any minute he was going to blow us to smithereens. I don't know what I thought.

Then there was Norma, Norma Jacoby, my editor at Bareback Books. It seems I'd missed several deadlines and Norma was up my ass day and night. I'd abandoned my Bareback Books work for *this* book, these pages that I'm writing at this moment, a book I was certain that no one would ever publish or read. Not smart, but I couldn't snap out of it. I knew I should have been doing my Norma work. I was dirt poor. I should have been making money, but I couldn't stop scribbling. It was a desperate period. I was sinking lower and lower. But I do have to say that Schvedchikov's industrial strength disinfectant sure cleared out my nasal passages like nobody's business. So I guess there's a good side to everything.

*O*ne of the enigmas I ponder in my solitude is—how the fuck could Doreen have fallen for a twirp like Harvey? I can understand why she left me, a failed writer, a roving jack of all trades. I mean, what could I have offered her? But Harvey! Jesus! If only it had been some guy from what you call a "good" family, if he'd gone to some fancy prep school like Choate or Andover, for example, or even West Point. If he'd been, say, a first lieutenant or even a second lieutenant, then sure, no problem. I could see why she'd prefer him over me, a truck driver who reads Latin and Greek, a busboy with a head full of Spinoza. But no! It had to be Harvey, an underclass lout who's every bit as much of a lowlife lumpen-proletariat goon as I am or worse. If only Harvey wasn't such a fucking twirp I could have felt...what? Better? Maybe, but just maybe. I wish you could see him, this fucking dyspeptic used car salesman from Bellflower with his monumental sense of entitlement and his stinking cigar and a jillion dandruff flakes stuck to his reading glasses. And him blinking like a myopic screech owl and puffing up his feathers. King of the roost, the bastard, I mean in his own eyes, and now as it turns out, in Doreen's eyes as well. And Bellflower, for Christ's sake! *Nobody* lives in Bellflower. Bellflower isn't a city, it's a strip mall. Why couldn't he have been from Paris or London or New York? Even Reykjavik! Shit! Shit! Shit! Harvey's a twirp! He *is* a twirp, he *was* a twirp, he *will be* a twirp! Well, fuck a duck. I can't...I can't go on with it. I can't...

*I*t didn't take my old Paris-days pal Hugo van der Weyden long to get up on his high horse after being adopted by the quality woman from Agoura Hills, or at least that's the way it seemed to me at first. Right after I moved in with Schvedchikov I got a postcard from Lisbon and one from Marrakech, and then a month or so later a letter postmarked West Palm Beach on mauve stationery, embossed and monogrammed, from "Hugo Michael van der Weyden." And when he called on Saturday, inviting me to Sunday brunch at the Beverly Hilton, there was something in his voice that I couldn't quite put my finger on, a note of condescension, I thought. Frankly, I was shocked—or dismayed, would be a better word. Even over the phone he seemed to be looking down his nose at me. But maybe, I told myself, you're becoming too sensitive.

Hugo fucking van der Weyden! It had been a long time. Hugo van der Weyden was like Starz in that he'd pop up every now and then, but there the resemblance ended. Unlike Starz, the middle-aged Rimbaud who roamed the world with just a toothbrush in his shirt pocket, Hugo van der Weyden was urbane, sophisticated and positively loaded with *savoir-faire*. Outrageously handsome, sleek and graceful, he'd captained the rowing team at Princeton and had a law degree as well as a PhD in psychology and an

AA in interior design. Back in the Paris days he'd published a book about High Renaissance art, and he'd been working forever on a biography of Oscar Wilde, but his main interest in life was women. Hugo van der Weyden was the sort of man who, because of his charm, poise, social status and all around good luck, frequently finds himself in a perfect position to offer comfort and companionship to women who...well, why not say it? He was a gigolo.

I caught a bus up Wilshire Boulevard. It was a beautiful Sunday morning, but I was feeling pretty uneasy. Just the same, I was determined to keep my appointment with Hugo because I had the idea now of hitting him up for a loan, a big loan, big enough to get me out of the sculptor's lair and into a furnished room somewhere, maybe up around the Fairfax district. And Hugo had the bling, no doubt about that. If he could afford brunch for two at the Beverly Hilton he could certainly afford to lend me a few hundred iron men.

A waiter led me to a table near the ice sculptures, caviar and prawns, and poured me a glass of champagne. Supposing Hugo didn't show? I didn't have enough money on me to cover even the tip. Sitting there at that table at the Beverly Hilton in my goodwill store clothes I felt like a beetle that had just crawled out from under the wallpaper. I gulped down my champagne, praying that the alcohol would brace me up. But when Hugo arrived, minutes later, I was pleasantly surprised. He'd changed, yes, but there was nothing high-handed about his manner. He was warm and effusive, and we hugged like the two old friends that we were and are. He was wearing a hand-painted tie, I noticed as he sat down opposite me, and his face, baked brick red by the Florida sun, looked like an expensive hothouse tomato.

"Donaldo! It's good to see you," he began, and after we'd hashed things over a bit I figured, *now*, yes, now's the time to hit him up, but before I could find the words he twinkled at me over the rim of his champagne glass and flashed that crooked lady-killer smile of his. "Listen, brother, have I got a deal for you. Your study, Donaldo, looks out on a white sand beach. A walnut roll top desk. It's an antique. The whole day free to write. You'll have your own split-level bathroom. And please understand, bro, you needn't decide anything right now. I just want to give you a general idea. The desk, by the way, is solid walnut. It's not a veneer. They didn't have veneer back in those days. This is a desk you can *write* on. It's huge. Plenty of elbow room."

"Sounds wonderful. What do I have to do? By the way, where's the little woman? I was hoping to meet her."

"Oh yeah, I'm sorry you couldn't meet Alexis. We're having some work done on the house in West Palm. I'll be joining her tomorrow in Nassau."

"Great! I'm happy for you. Now...the walnut desk? You were saying? Roll top, you say?"

"Right, right. But first let me ask you this, Donaldo." He leans across the table, studying me keenly with narrowed eyes while nervously drumming his fingers on the tablecloth. "How do you feel about dating a woman who has a prosthetic limb?" When I didn't answer he snapped his fingers and continued. "On second thought, forget that. There's this other woman I want to introduce you to. A very special woman. You've heard of Jupiter Island? The homes of the stars? It's near West Palm. Donald Trump has a mansion out there. This lady's name is Mrs. Ariel Peggoty-Smythe. She's looking for a male companion."

"Look, Hugo, I'm afraid I'm hardly the sort of man... I mean, if she's so rich, why not some handsome young guy?"

"She's tried that. The beautiful boys. She wants somebody she can *talk* to."

"I don't know..."

"Look, my friend, I'm offering you a chance to move

up the ladder. It's no wonder you've had such rotten luck with women. I mean, after some of the trash you've taken up with. You don't mind my saying that, do you? Mrs. Ariel Peggoty-Smythe is different. She's not your usual run of sailor-girls. This woman exudes class. She's absolutely unique, she's the crème de la crème, she's—"

"Extra virgin?"

"Now you're getting the idea! What do you say?"

My thoughts were racing as I tried to frame the question about the loan. It was all going down too quickly. In my mind I could hear that demon refrigerator ticking, proclaiming the inexorable march of time and the ephemeral quality of human life. I could see by now exactly what Hugo was getting at. He wanted to put me up for adoption, and I knew he meant well, but I had a different scenario in mind. I'd get the loan and I'd move into that furnished room in the Fairfax district, maybe on North Orange Grove Avenue or Rosewood. There was a little park on Rosewood, I recalled, so beautiful and green in summer when the lawn sprinklers are twirling and joyful kids are tossing Frisbees, and I could walk to Canter's Deli from there. A furnished room in the home of a nice Jewish lady, and she'd bring me a warm bagel with cream cheese in the morning. A sunny garret room, most likely, facing west, and I'd look out my window while I typed... That was the life I wanted, sedate, orderly, decorous. The writer's life. I'm a man of letters for Christ's sake, not an edge city desperado! And all I needed to make it happen was money. Money, money, money. I plucked up my courage. How about now? No, not while he's talking, you idiot. Don't interrupt him. On the other hand, why wait? Can't you hear that clock ticking? This is my life that's slipping away, goddamn it! Always too timid. Timid, timid, timid. Why couldn't I have had a regular Type A personality? *Take names and kick ass!* Instead, I'm the Amoeba Man. Okay...*now!* Now, while he's slurping down that oyster. Don't think; just let the words come out.

"Listen, Hugo, there's something else I'd like to..."

"Wait! Let me finish, will you? Hear me out, and then you can decide. I don't know if I mentioned this, but she's a huge art buff. You two will have a lot to talk about. She has an original Degas at her place on Jupiter Island. *Jupiter Island, Donaldo!* It's a writer's paradise. *Seventeen miles of private beach!* Burt Reynolds has a mansion out there. And Dan Marino. You're going to write the Great American Novel!"

"And she just wants to talk, you say."

"Donaldo, the woman... She's a *human being.* She wants conversation, companionship. I don't want to mislead you here, my friend. She *will* expect a certain amount of..."

"Of?"

"Well, of...of...*playtime.*"

By the time Hugo had finished his pitch we were having coffee and my chance had fled. I couldn't very well ask him for a loan after turning down his proposal, could I?

Back at the Minotaur's lair I sat on my bunk and watched a cockroach run rapidly up the wall and disappear behind a Rolling Stones poster as I reflected on my meeting with Hugo. I'd failed miserably in my mission to hit Hugo up for a loan, but it had been good to see my old pal, and he hadn't changed all that much, I realized. He was the same old Hugo van der Weyden under a rather appealing surface layer of newly acquired glitz and glamour.

I got up, made my way through the labyrinth to the fridge and cracked open a 40-ounce King Cobra. Cockroaches, they say, can go for a month without food, and they can survive on such meager fare as the glue from the back of a postage stamp. *My God, a walnut roll top desk...* I suppose I passed up a golden opportunity, but what the hell. I'm a survivor. Let's see...by now Hugo should be boarding the plane for Nassau. They'll be staying at the Wyndham, he said, then after a bit of island hopping, snorkeling and sunbathing, they'll scoot over to Miami where they'll board the *Norwegian Epic for* a 15-day transatlantic cruise to Marseilles and Barcelona. I'm happy for Hugo. It's a wonderful life for him. A world of privilege and luxury—exotic ports of call, five star hotels, fine dining and the finest wines. All that will be his—for as long as his pecker holds up.

Looking back, the business with Doreen, that was nothing more than recreational crucifixion. Fact is, I enjoyed it. Let's face it; one develops a taste for suffering. But Marlena now, that was the real thing. Not only the *peine forte et dure* but also a transformative experience. Marlena reduced me to a molecule; she transformed me into an amoeba. I tried my best to hang on, a polyp clinging to the wall of her uterus, but when the pull of the moon was right she opened the sluice gates and flushed me out on the crest of a bloodstained tide. That was supposed to destroy me, send me spinning out of the world, but it only succeeded in making me frisky as hell and practically invisible. After Marlena I became a flyspeck, an atom, a pipsqueak so microscopic that any number of me could dance on the head of a pin. I'm dancing now, in fact, I'm dancing the amoeba-dance, light as a feather on my ten thousand pseudopodia. I like being a nothing. Nor do I have any intention of growing arms and legs, and especially not a heart. It's too messy. I have to laugh, really. If the world suspected that I'm still clinging to its dirty hide like a tick, fattening myself on its precious blood, it would flick me off with a swish of its flea-bitten tail, no question about that. But I'm what you call a resistant strain. I eat DDT for breakfast and E.coli for lunch. I'm a tiny spark of light in the darkness. I have not been extinguished.

9

"As I was walking among the fires of hell..." A hot Santa Ana wind blowing in from the desert inspired an all-night gabfest with Fausto and Cliff English at Sol Fingerbein's studio on Seventh Street downtown near the Orpheum Theater. Helped along by great gulps of dry-as-dust Gallo pinot noir, we pitched into William Blake's apocalyptic writings, including *The Bible of Hell*.

In the early morning hours when the wine was gone and Sol Fingerbein was asleep at his easel, and Cliff and Fausto were at last winding down, I left the studio, heading for Maria's at Grand Central Market.

Walking... Sixth Street. It's almost daylight now and I've got menudo on my mind, a steaming bowl of menudo with plenty of oregano, chopped onion and cilantro and a squeeze of lime. And corn tortillas, of course, *tortillas de maíz*. At the same time I'm thinking about a tourist girl, a Minnesota blonde, whiter than white and innocent as an apple fritter, she stopped me yesterday on Hollywood Boulevard and asked directions to Grauman's Chinese. When I pointed it out, just blocks away, she exclaimed proudly, "Billy Graham has a star there now! Did you know that?" After pretending to cogitate for a moment I was obliged to confess that I didn't. We talked briefly, and when she learned that I was a writer she snapped my photo and asked me if I knew the Beach Boys and Jennifer Aniston.

Walking... Fifth Street: the runic graffiti, the cardboard villages, the medieval squalor. At dawn the city regurgitates its masticated prey, blackened faces raked by spiked teeth, the ragtag horde, these half human chiggers and bedbugs that infest God's clean limbs. You'd be doing these poor blighted bastards a favor if you mounted a thirty-caliber machinegun on a tripod and chopped them up like so much sausage meat.

That Santa Ana wind, it not only makes you crazy, it makes you nostalgic. I can remember when skid row in Los Angeles was a chummy sort of place. You could find friends there, you could have a drink with a bona-fide Fifth Street wino. Now it's a refugee camp, a cellblock, the Ninth Circle of Hell. Look at those scarecrows huddled around that smoldering trash barrel, scratching themselves like apes in a zoo. They'll kill you for your shoes up in this motherfucker. Go home Minnesota! This isn't any Walk of Fame church supper down here, darling. It makes me sick to think of grimy hands, the fingers shiny with ground-in dirt, on your little white teacup ass. Run, Minnesota, run like hell, cover your tracks, burn your high school yearbook, tear up your drivers license, dye your hair, change your name, hide under the bed and pray they don't find you. There's nothing for you here, girl. Billy Graham can't save us now, and neither can the baby Jesus. The angels have poured out their vials; the rivers have turned to blood and the sea has turned to warm piss.

Later. It's 8am and I'm standing at the top of the Bunker Hill steps with a belly full of menudo, looking out over the city, a mirror glass world of reflections lost in reflections. Nothing like menudo to settle you down after a night of drinking. Menudo gives you weight, it gives you balance, it gives you *gravitas*. I'm thinking about the Apocalypse. Is everything on schedule, I wonder? Will the Apocalypse come hurtling up on steel wheels, showering us with sparks and hissing jets of live steam? Will there be faces in the sky, and will they be weeping? Will there be angels with great shimmering wings, waving tambourines and cartridge belts? Will there be candy soldiers with melted guns, whose coffins are newspaper boats harnessed to swans? Will we fry on the pavement like strips of bacon, or will we simply dissolve—like tigers—into beautiful golden mush? Will...

*T*he Santa Ana wind moved out and September arrived, bringing with it a welcome coolness, and the viscous machine-oil stench of the smog seemed to conceal a hint of rain. I was down to my last five bucks and I was determined to blow it on a good breakfast—huevos rancheros, papas fritas and corn tortillas at La Pachanga. As I hoofed it past Lafayette Park a grimy woman in a dirty burlap dress called to me from a narrow alley: "You want my *poosey?*" As if to avoid any chance of ambiguity in the matter she pulled up her dress, revealing her furry treasure. I nodded a curt hello and kept going, but she persisted, running after me, frightening me a little. I mean, in LA you never know. It was beginning to rain and I was so impatient to get the hell out of there that I simply reached in my pocket and handed the woman my last five-dollar bill. She scurried like a spider back to her lair and I thought that was the end of it, but before I could continue walking she flopped down on a big sheet of cardboard next to a dumpster and spread her legs as an eerie flash of lightning lit up the alley. "*Don't you want my poosey?*" she shrieked in a voice strangled with tears. Huge raindrops spattered on the sidewalk, and it seemed to me that the sky was weeping as I turned and walked, head down, into the driving rain.

I was so unnerved by now that it was only after I'd

reached La Pachanga and ducked inside out of the downpour that I realized I'd just given away my last five bucks and there'd be no *huevos rancheros* for me, and no *tortillas de maiz*. I didn't have enough for even a coffee.

I drifted back over toward Lafayette Park. The rain had stopped. I didn't have anything particular in mind. My stomach wanted to eat. At the park I ran into Roderick, the homeless philosophy professor, and Mad Rosa the Flower Lady. Roderick—charismatic, professorial—had managed to corral a well-heeled tourist couple and a meal was in the offing.

One of Roderick's favorite yarns was the story of the Freakmaker, which he claimed he'd first heard years ago in Paris from the lips of a man named Grobbel. We sat on a bench near the Marquis de Lafayette statue, the tourists, Mad Rosa and me, while Roderick paced up and down and dug in his overcoat pocket for a flat bottle of Ancient Age as he summoned the words. I'd already heard the story, of course, and Mad Rosa understood only a little English, but the tourist couple, Tom and Marge, were all ears.

"I never should have allowed Grobbel to accompany me to dinner that night at Marcel Artaud's," Roderick began. "But Grobbel... Grobbel desperately needed a decent meal and Marcel Artaud, generous guy that he was, told me: 'A writer? Sure, bring him along.'

"It was Paris, 1959. I was a student at the Sorbonne, and I was having trouble making ends meet. I was sleeping, in fact, in a wine cellar in Montmartre. Marcel Artaud lived nearby. Artaud was a pastiche artist, and extremely successful. His work was collage, pasted fabric, also leather. I will say this: it meant nothing whatever to me. Still I thought we might hit it off, as friends, and the truth is, we did. Our evenings, at dinner and after, were delightful, even Biblical, as I often commented, with Naomi sitting at the harp, a concert grand, while Marcel and I discussed one thing and another over a glass or two of fins bois cognac.

"The Artauds were middle-aged, more than twenty years my senior, but that never matter at all. Naomi baked her own bread, and she always sent a loaf home with me, Old World rye or sometimes Russian *culibac,* a wonderful creation stuffed with chopped cabbage, onions and seasoned ground beef..."

"The Artauds..." I prompted. I was hungry as a wolf and I didn't want Roderick going on and on about food, as he had a tendency to do.

"Yes, of course, the Artauds. Marcel Artaud was extremely bright, a cultured man, erudite to say the least. He spoke Russian and Yiddish, and we shared many interests. He knew his way around the Old Testament, I can tell you that. We'd often talk in great detail about Joseph's sojourn in Egypt and his interpretation of Pharaoh's dreams. Another favorite topic was the monumental translation of the King James Version of the Bible in 1611 and the intriguing if apocryphal story that Shakespeare was called in to touch up the Book of Isaiah. An artist he wasn't, Marcel Artaud—he was more of an interior decorator—but he was an excellent companion and a thoroughly decent man.

"Marcel Artaud had invited me into his studio, into his home, and I felt very grateful for this. But I must confess that having gained the confidence of this man, having entered his world, if only into the vestibule thereof, that the foremost thought in my mind was: can I hit this joker up for a loan? I was desperate. I didn't know how I was going to eat, and yet I wanted to go on with my studies. It was cold, bitter cold in my wine cellar in Montmartre, and there were rats."

"What about Grobbel? You mentioned a man named Grobbel..."

"Tom, stop interrupting," Marge exclaimed.

"Marge, I'm just... Please, go ahead, Roderick."

"Grobbel, yes, I was coming to that. Grobbel... How to explain Grobbel? The phrase 'warped brilliance' comes readily to mind. Grobbel was an American, an unpublished poet who was both unable and unwilling to confine his antisocial impulses to his art. He had to have it out with people. An intellectual's disdain for the herd, a savage contempt for anyone who wasn't an artist—that was Grobbel. Just as I today have no regular address, so it was in those days with Grobbel. He camped on the floors of friends' apartments in Montmartre, or more often, he slept on the Metro, a risky practice, but Grobbel was well over six feet tall, and due to the irrepressible hostility which he projected, he appeared to be—and was—a dangerous man.

"I thought, wrongly, that in allowing Grobbel to accompany me that night, I was accomplishing a double purpose. One, I would secure for my pal Grobbel a square meal, something he desperately needed. Two, by having him along, an intellectual, articulate, knowledgeable, I would show Marcel Artaud, by way of softening him up for the hoped-for loan, that I was a person of substance, a serious man, a student of life, if you will.

"But Grobbel didn't want anything good to happen to him, and, by extension, he didn't want anything good to happen to me. He wanted to suffer, and he wanted me to suffer, that was the long and short of it. And so, after we'd put away a delicious meal, and after Grobbel had reviewed Marcel Artaud's facile collages, the cold contempt and sneering disdain which Grobbel found so easy to express began to surface. I was humiliated and I was furious, both with Grobbel and with myself. Grobbel, as I should have foreseen, was blind to the goodness that emanated from these two charming and kind-hearted people. And so Grobbel did what he'd so often done, at seemingly propitious social engagements in the past: he told the story of the Freakmaker.

"Always Grobbel began this chilling story with an impressive list of credentials. The tale had been recorded, so he said, by a princess of the Hapsburg Dynasty. It was purportedly a true history that featured her mother,

Melissandra of Avignon, as the heroine. It was written, of course, in Latin, presumably dictated to a scribe, since most women at that time, even those of noble birth, were illiterate. The account was translated into French by Jean de Vignay in his *Miroir Historial* in 1348, the same year that the young Princess Joan, daughter of Edward III, died of the plague near Bordeaux after setting off at the tender age of thirteen to marry Pedro the Cruel of Castile. The story was also included, Grobbel maintained, in Froissart's *Chroniques de France et d'Angleterre*. I should mention, however, that years later, out of curiosity, I consulted Froissart in the New York Public Library and found no mention there of Melissandra of Avignon. Thus it's possible that Grobbel made the story up out of whole cloth. If so, it was a masterful piece of legerdemain.

"There was also a portrait, Grobbel insisted, of Melissandra of Avignon, from the hand of no less a master than Giotto, painted in the year 1321. The Giotto original was unfortunately lost or destroyed, but not before it was copied by one of the Van Eyck brothers in 1439. The Van Eyck portrait underwent a tortuous course through the centuries, finally to become the property of Luftwaffe General Josef Kammhuber. It was destroyed in the Thousand-Bomber Raid on Cologne in May, 1942. Very elaborate, these credentials, and, as I say, very impressive.

"Once he'd gained his listeners' undivided attention with this mesmerizing display of erudition, Grobbel would go on to deliver the story of the Freakmaker in point-blank fashion, a performance which never failed to evoke both disgust and dismay. After Grobbel had thoroughly chilled his listeners with this epic of deformity—for such it was— while simultaneously enthralling them, he reveled in his perverse triumph. Like a spider that transfixes some hapless insect and binds it with an intricate web, Grobbel, having performed these preliminary maneuvers par excellence, took great delight in embalming his victims with his own special brand of deadening venom.

"But the story... Garrick the Freakmaker, a miser—he was a hunchback, according to Grobbel—went about in rags. He didn't want anyone to know he was rich. His money he kept in a sump in the floor of the subterranean dungeon beneath the narrow crooked streets of medieval Paris, the habitat that he shared with his creations.

"Numerous odd-shaped giant glass bottles, the contours of which determined the deformity of their inhabitants, were arranged on pallets set in neat rows in this chamber of horrors not far from the Cathedral of Notre Dame.

"The Freakmaker fed his captives through the open neck of the bottle with a kind of long-handled forceps. The bottom of each bottle was in the form of a grated floor upon which the maturing freak stood and which permitted the passing of urine and excrement. For a bath, Garrick simply dumped a pitcher of water into the neck of the bottle and let it flow over the malformed mass of human flesh contained therein.

"Thus, day after day, year after year, in this horrific potato cellar beneath the streets of Paris, the bottled freaks matured, becoming, with the passage of time, more and more intriguingly disfigured due to the odd contours of the bottles in which they were imprisoned, and consequently, more and more salable, more and more an expressly viable commodity, more and more a supremely marketable item.

"At night the Freakmaker lay down on his pallet of straw. Against the piteous cries of his charges he stuffed his ears with beeswax. In a world without radios, telephones or television, the dungeon was blessedly silent, except for the sound of drizzling water and nameless filth pouring down from the cobbled street above and the ceaseless scraping and scampering of rat feet.

"The Freakmaker obtained his victims for a pittance. Often they were children stolen and sold by Gypsies, even the children of Gypsies themselves. Or, since at the time peasants, having no other recourse against famine, were frequently obliged to sell their children, they were the offspring of the poor, these pitiful products of the soil.

"The Freakmaker received huge fees for his creations. His vintage freaks were very much in demand in the royal courts of Europe, where it must be said in all fairness that these monstrosities were assured of being kept, in many cases, in grand style. Curiously misshapen girls, for example, who had developed a sweet perfection of form analogous to the finish a great claret, were especially marketable to noblemen whose refined palates demanded unusual sensual delights."

"Good God!"

"Tom, stop interrupting!"

"The bottled children either died, went mad, or developed extraordinarily strong characters. Those of the first category didn't last long. They languished and died of a broken heart or of a broken spirit or both. The Freakmaker had no recourse but to write them off as a loss. He buried the bodies of the ruined children in a common grave beneath the dungeon floor.

"Child prisoners of the second category, unable to endure the inhuman conditions of their incarceration, sought escape in madness. Their minds became as misshapen as their bodies. Far from detracting from their marketability, the mental aberrations of these tortured creatures placed them in particular demand in the royal courts of Europe because the gentlefolk found their antics amusing.

"Freaks of the third category, those who developed strong characters, frequently became court jesters and displayed an amazing facility with musical instruments, particularly the violin, undoubtedly due in large part to the unimaginable suffering they had endured. The souls of these stunted creatures had blossomed, *faute de mieux*, like tropical flowers."

"Incredible...heartbreaking...please go on."

"To the third category belonged Melissandra of

Avignon, the subject of the curious history allegedly written by her daughter. This extraordinary woman may have been a Spanish Gypsy, but since she had been kidnapped and sold into slavery while still a young child, she had, according to the history, no recollection of her origin.

"As Melissandra matured in her bottle, attended by Garrick the Freakmaker, who lavished upon her the full complement of his vintner's skill, she began to display a strange and haunting beauty, as well as a singularly compelling force of personality. With her white skin, raven hair and enormous black eyes, made luminous by suffering, and her lopsided body—stunted, crab-like, yet possessed of an eerie and enthrallingly grotesque beauty—she managed quite easily to thoroughly enchant her captor while she was still, so to speak, *in vitro*.

"Utterly bewitched, Garrick exchanged his filthy rags for a sporty tattersall vest, a velvet tunic, an ermine-fringed robe and pointed shoes of variegated colors. He arranged his wispy hair on his bulging forehead in comical spit curls. Much older than she, he hovered around his bottled tête de cuvée troll queen in humpbacked glee, displaying all of the foolishness which December invariably exhibits under the amorous spell of May.

"Infatuated beyond all bounds, and very much the *sommelier* in his laughable grotesqueries, the Freakmaker adored Melissandra through the thick glass, dreaming in his hunchbacked dreams of the magical day when he would at last break the bottle containing his adored ogress and inhale her exquisite bouquet.

"Garrick's infatuation with Melissandra proved to be his undoing. Ironically, as Grobbel never failed to point out, the evil Freakmaker's downfall was brought about by the only decent act of his life. He released Melissandra from her bottle. A priest of sorts was brought down into the rat-infested dungeon, and the hunchback and the gourd-shaped maiden were joined in a brief private ceremony.

"For several weeks following her release and her forced marriage to the hunchback Melissandra exhibited a terrifying strength of will. With masterful aplomb she feigned affection for her gaoler and freely engaged in sexual relations with him until she had gained his confidence and learned the location of his buried treasure-hoard. On the very next night, after Garrick had enjoyed her banjo-shaped body and lay quiescent in her arms, Melissandra plunged a dagger into his hump and subsequently she unceremoniously slit the stricken man's throat.

"There followed, according to Grobbel, a frenzy of rage and repressed anger. Melissandra seized a hammer and ran amuck through the dungeon, randomly smashing the bottles of the incarcerated freaks, the lumpish and malformed oddities that had been her companions in misfortune. The bewildered creatures, many of them bleeding from superficial or even life-threatening cuts and lacerations, wandered out into the crooked darkened streets of medieval Paris, never to be heard from again.

"Grobbel sometimes added at this juncture the following detail regarding the Van Eyck copy of the original Giotto portrait of Melissandra of Avignon: that whoever so much as looked upon the portrait of this extraordinary woman with her Quasimodesque body, her *blancs de blancs* complexion and her hypnotic gaze, fell immediately and irrevocably under her spell.

"Following the death of Garrick the Freakmaker, and a trial for murder, from which she emerged victorious, Melissandra went on to build several sumptuous chateaux financed by the hunchback's treasure, one in Avignon, another in Hamburg, and a third in the Hanseatic city of Danzig. Subsequently she lived on a grand style, mingling freely with nobility, buoyed up and carried forward not merely by her newfound wealth, but also by the irresistible force and magnetism of her personality, as well as her extraordinary appearance.

"She married, as the history shows, a prince of the Hapsburgs, and lived a rich and fulfilling life. There were born to her numerous sons and daughters, all of them normal, and one of these daughters—according to Grobbel—wrote the history which I've just related. I should add, as Grobbel sometimes did, in certain versions of his tale, that there was also a child born to Melissandra of her union with Garrick the Freakmaker, an exceptionally beautiful child, a perfectly normal baby girl. She killed it."

"My God, Roderick," Tom muttered. "That's quite a story."

"Yes, well, you can thank Melissandra of Avignon—or Grobbel."

And with that Roderick deftly steered the lot of us across the street to La Pachanga for *pollo encebollado* and *plátanos fritos* washed down with Carta Blanca beer. Roderick and I were both famished and we waded into the food with gusto while Mad Rosa grinned foolishly and ate with her fingers.

"But Roderick, what about the artist and his wife?" Marge asked as she speared a fried banana with her fork. "How did they react, I mean, when Grobbel finished his..." nbsp; "His epic of disfigurement? You mean the Artauds? Well, they were stunned, as you may imagine. Naomi sat at her harp, utterly immobilized. Not single lilting note came from her fingers. Marcel, aghast, bewildered, numbed, stared wordlessly at his half-finished glass of cognac. Finally, without looking up, he muttered something like, '*Well, it's been a wonderful evening...*'

"Without a word I stood up and walked out the door, with Grobbel close behind. Snow was falling in Montmartre. The wind was howling. The streets were desolate. As we pounded the pavement in silence Grobbel kept grinning at me slyly as if he expected to be congratulated for having achieved a resounding success.

When, to my huge relief, he ducked like a scarecrow into a Metro entrance, I didn't bother to look at him or say good night. My feet were freezing. Slush was seeping into my torn sneakers. Alone, chilled, dead broke, I leaned into the wind, heading for my wine cellar and another night of bone-cold shivering."

10

Roderick disappeared for a while after that, and then one day just before Christmas I saw him sitting on a bench in MacArthur Park next to the Hungarian Freedom Fighters obelisk. He'd exchanged his 43rd Infantry overcoat for a Navy pea coat but he was still wearing his crumpled Borsalino and he'd grown a Confederate general's flowing gray beard. And his unalienable air of entitlement hadn't deserted him; I saw that clearly enough as I stood for a moment gazing at him—I mean the way he sprawled on his bench, legs apart, collar turned up, as relaxed and casual as if he were sitting in his own living room. He was the prince of the city; it all belonged to him; he was a grand duke gazing out the window of his manor and MacArthur Park was his lawn, the greensward of his estate.

"Donaldo," he murmured as he looked up and saw me. I hurried over; he stood up; we embraced. He'd been feeding the pigeons but his birdseed was almost gone so he suggested that we head over to La Pachanga for a beer and a bite to eat. I was flat broke so I said I had a meeting with my editor (not true) because I didn't want to be riding along on the coattails of a homeless man who needed every penny he could scrape, but Roderick somehow divined my thoughts and insisted that I accompany him because, as he said, "You're my best friend in this town." This town, because, as I learned, it was Roderick's custom to hop a freight from time to time and spend a month or two in San Francisco or Seattle, or New York in the summer, or New Orleans or another town in the sunny south when the weather turned cold in California. He'd lived just about everywhere and he knew America as well as any long haul truck driver.

As we were passing the legendary Park Plaza Hotel with its massive neogothic angels who have gazed out over MacArthur Park since 1925, apparently unperturbed by the million or so drug deals they've seen go down, Roderick suggested that instead of going to La Pachanga we visit his former colleague, Dr. John Van Rysselberge, a retired professor who'd taught English Lit at Berkeley. "I'm staying with him for a while, and I'd like you to meet him. He's an urban recluse, something of a fussbudget and I suppose some might say a stuffy old fart, but he's got quite a head on his shoulders, and I can guarantee you he's read just about everything. I mean, he's a huge Spengler fan, *Decline of the West*, and he's written a couple of books, too, on film noir, I think. And a biography of Dulcibella Stolzenberg, if I'm not mistaken. Anyway, he's a wonderful host and an excellent conversationalist, and best of all, he's a marvelous cook. Well, you'll see. You're in for a real treat, my friend!"

Since the way to my heart is through my stomach I agreed, and we caught a bus to the Professor's digs on Normandie, a tree-lined street of palatial homes.

The lugubrious chiming of the doorbell reminded me of a funeral parlor, but when Professor Van Rysselberge appeared at the door in a crisp white apron and I smelled a heavenly fragrance emanating presumably from the kitchen I knew I'd come to the right place. "What is it?" I asked the Professor, as soon as we'd shaken hands. "That you're cooking? I can't...quite place..."

"Marinated leg of venison." The Professor was a small thin man with sad blue eyes. He seemed to be standing on tiptoes. "You're not a vegetarian, I hope. But let's go into the kitchen and have a look, shall we?"

As elegant as the Professor's house was on the outside, inside it was like a warehouse, a warehouse filled with books, towering stacks of books, some of which leaned dangerously as our tiptoeing host led us along a narrow aisle between the book stacks. Professor Van Rysselberge was an urban recluse, all right—very much like Schvedchikov.

"The Professor seems sort of...sad," I whispered to Roderick as we fell back a pace or two.

"He's read far too many books," Roderick muttered confidentially. "Knowledge is sorrow, my friend. Knowledge is sorrow. You know, this is something you might want to consider yourself. I notice you always have a book under your arm. On the other hand, don't mind me. Old men are famous for giving bad advice."

The kitchen was spacious. Gleaming pots and pans dangled from the ceiling and an enormous wooden butcher's block squatted in the center of the room. The Professor popped open the oven and gave us a mouth-watering whiff of the sizzling leg of venison, then, with maitre d-like aplomb, he reeled off a list of the side dishes that would be accompanying the roast.

"We'll be starting out with crab bisque, and...well I hope you like stuffed mushrooms...and I put some shallots and macadamia nuts in the salad, and with the venison we're having fingerling potatoes and asparagus... But let's go into my study where we can talk."

"My God, what's the occasion?" I whispered to Roderick as the Professor led us through another narrow rabbit run between stacks of books.

"You mean the menu? Nothing," Roderick muttered. "He's lonely. Locked up in here, as you see, with his books...for years, decades. Cooking fills his hours. He went to chef's school in Stockholm before he became an English professor."

In the study—a padded cell insulated by walls of books—the Professor showed us a photo of himself as a young man in a low-slung British sports car, a trip through Scandinavia where he met his Swedish wife who had died ten years ago in a skiing accident at St. Moritz.

The Professor offered us some homemade glögg— pronounced "gloog"—hot spiced wine, the traditional Scandinavian Christmas drink, a favorite of his deceased Swedish wife, Birgitta. He spelled it out for us, "glögg," umlaut and all, and then he told us how you make the stuff. "You start with a bottle of red wine, add a quart of brandy and some sugar, and then the spices, cardamom, cinnamon, cloves, raisins, almonds, figs..." The list of ingredients went on and on, a hell of a thing to do to a bottle of red wine, in my opinion, and besides I'm scary of drinking anything signified by a word with an umlaut.

Nevertheless, I couldn't very well refuse. The Professor poured. *"Skål!"*

"*Skål*!" Roderick and I responded in unison.

After a tentative gulp of glögg I picked up a book, *Mount Analogue* by René Daumal. The Professor's blue eyes fixed me sharply. "*Mount Analogue*. You've read *Mount Analogue?*"

"*Mount Analogue?* Sure, yes, of course. René Daumal."

"René Daumal, Gurdjieff's pupil..."

"Yes. Gurdjieff, Alexandre de Salzmann..."

"My God, man, we have a lot to discuss!"

But the three of us sat down in comfortable chairs and almost immediately the conversation veered to a discussion of film noir.

"The classic noir films were subversive," the Professor began. "They questioned the facade of everyday life in movies that had wide appeal. Films noir are about the individual in a hostile universe, typically an anti-hero who has, let's say, one last shot at redemption. As you probably know, there's a theory that the genesis of film noir originates in post World War II trauma, but I think we have to look to an earlier period. In my opinion, film noir was a manifestation of the fear, the despair and above all the loneliness we find at the core of American life, I mean, well before Pearl Harbor and Hiroshima and all of that. By the way," he said, turning to me, "how do you like the glögg?"

"Fantastic," I chirped, trying to screw my face up in a semblance of a smile. The stuff might as well have been horse piss, but I'd managed to choke most of it down. After all I was a guest and then there was the business about the deceased Swedish wife and whatnot.

"The noir genre actually emerged before America entered World War II," the Professor went on. "I'm talking about the émigré European directors and cinematographers who fashioned a totally new kind of cinema from the gangster films of the 30's and the pre-War detective novels of writers like Raymond Chandler and Dashiell Hammett. We can also clearly see the influence of German expressionism, you know, and the burgeoning knowledge of Freudian and Jungian psychology, as well as precursors in the French poetic realist films of the 30's. Noir was...how shall I say it? Noir was about the shadow, the dark self, and the alienation in the modern American city that manifests itself in psychosis, criminality, and paranoia. Many of the great European directors that landed in Hollywood were fleeing fascism, you know, and had leftist views. While the popular critique of the intellectual left of Europe was a response to existentialism, the response of others was an inclination to nihilism, and we can see nihilism too in many noirs of the classic cycle. But I'm forgetting..."

The Professor hopped nimbly to his feet and tiptoed out of the room. He returned a moment later with a silver pitcher. Beaming proudly, he refilled our goblets with hot spiced glögg or gloog or whatever.

"*Skål!*

I was already pretty well hammered. It must have been the brandy on an empty stomach—or the cardamom, or the cinnamon or the cloves—and I had to take a leak. After the mandatory clinking of the glasses and the gulping of the glögg, Professor Van Rysselberge muttered, "Let me see now, where was I?"

My back teeth were floating but I didn't feel that I should excuse myself just as the Professor was about to resume his monologue. "Nihilism," I prompted.

"Ah, yes, nihilism. I'm afraid that life in the shadows has made a nihilist out of me. This solitude, you know, I mean, being alone so much, alone with my books, and especially, I mean, after Birgitta's passing. But I think there's a lot of confusion in the popular mind as to exactly what nihilism is. Nihilism is viewed as something dark, negative and evil, but this isn't necessarily the case. For example, nihilism *chez moi* is merely a rejection of politics, religion, art, music, literature, philosophy, ethics and morality. Other than that, it's a wholehearted affirmation of life. And this kind of nihilism is precisely why the films of the classic noir directors have such a lasting appeal: they dispense with the bric-a-brac, the meaningless cultural detritus with which civilized people surround themselves and they zero in on the essential *beingness* of the individual."

"Would you excuse me, please," I ventured, lurching to my feet. "I need to..."

"The lavabo? Right down the hall." And he told me which aisles between the book stacks to follow—and it must have been the glögg or the gloog—I mean I was slipping and sliding like an epileptic on ice skates—but I could swear he instructed me to turn right at Dickens, left at Dostoevsky and then take another hard left at the intersection of Oswald Spengler and Giambattista Vico.

The bathroom, predictably, was well stocked with books and magazines—a regular library. Myself, I've never understood this proclivity for bathroom reading that some people have. You do your business and you get out. That's my idea of it. But recently I saw on the Internet that the Marquis de Sade wrote *The 120 Days of Sodom* on a 40-foot roll of toilet paper while he was a prisoner in the Bastille. So maybe I've been wrong all these years. Not about reading in the toilet, exactly, but rather, maybe if I'd *written* in the toilet, maybe if I'd written my books on a roll of toilet paper, I would have had better luck. Or maybe if my mother hadn't smashed my father's mandolin and I'd learned to play an instrument of some kind. Well, the hell with it.

The dinner began with piping hot crab bisque served with fragrant, paper-thin slices of venison prosciutto, stuffed mushrooms and a tangy whole grain mustard remoulade, followed by a wonderful crisp romaine salad liberally sprinkled with garlic foccacia croutons, Sonoma goat cheese, shallots and candied macadamia nuts. We ate in the kitchen, sitting around the massive maple butcher block.

"Extraordinary," Roderick commented as he munched an arugula leaf. "The macadamia nuts...beyond compare..."

"*Gourmet Magazine*," the Professor admitted blushingly.

The Venison roast with a caramelized shallot demiglace was served with fingerling potatoes, sautéed heirloom tomatoes and baby carrots with miso-honey beurre blanc. We washed it all down with a hearty Bordeaux, but the gloog had already done its devilish work, and I was reeling drunk by the time we pitched into the crème brûlée. It had been a great meal and what I desperately needed now was a snooze, but it suddenly occurred to me that I would have to ask the Professor for bus fare if I was to get back home—an awkward business to say the least. As I was mulling this conundrum over in my mind, Professor Van Rysselberge, apparently reading my thoughts, suggested that, since it was now quite late, I spend the night in one of the guest rooms.

"I can't tell you how happy it makes me having a writer stay here with me," the Professor explained as he led me up the stairs. We were both on tippy-toes now (for some reason I felt that I had to imitate the Professor's walk). "I don't get many visitors, you know," he continued in a confidential tone. "And we still have to talk, you and I, about Gurdjieff and René Daumal and Alexandre de Salzmann... My God, that was such a fertile period. You've read Ouspensky, of course. *In Search of the Miraculous?*"

"Yes, yes..."

My room was delightful. As we stepped inside a breeze stirred the curtains bringing with it the aroma of star jasmine, and on the dresser I spied a framed photo of a young woman—almost certainly Birgitta—perched on the fender of the low-slung British sports car.

"If you need anything..." the Professor murmured as he turned to leave, but now that a bed for the night was assured I began feeling a bit more feisty and I allowed the Professor to persuade me to come back downstairs for a final cup of coffee and glass of Chartreuse. Roderick, the Professor informed me, was camping in a pup tent in the back yard. There were any number of guest rooms available, but Roderick, he explained, preferred to sleep outdoors whenever possible. "He's one of a kind," the Professor murmured reverently as we rejoined Roderick in the kitchen. "The last of the American hoboes..."

The coffee was served just the way I like it, Mexican *café de vaso* style, made with hot milk instead of water, and the absinth-green Chartreuse, curiously enough, had something of a sobering effect on me, meaning that instead of blind stinking drunk I was now just pleasantly blotto. And I liked the way the Professor deftly resumed his monologue, picking up right where he'd left off, instead of letting the conversation degenerate into drunken chitchat.

"My interest in film noir has been just a part of my ongoing effort to understand just how and when the current malaise infected us, when it began, this ennui, you know, this soul sickness that characterizes modern American life in this century, our century."

"You're writing a book, Professor?" I put in.

"Please, call me John. Yes, yes...ha ha, I'm afraid so."

"Don't be so modest, John," Roderick interjected. "I've read some of it, Donald, and it's a blockbuster. He's going to give Spengler a run for his money."

"Please, Roderick. I hardly expect to blow *Decline of the West* out of the water. By the way, *'Decline of the West'* is a pretty insipid translation, wouldn't you say, Donald, of *Der Untergang Des Abendlandes?* I mean...*Untergang!* Now there's a word with muscle. You don't have to understand German to know what *'Untergang'* means, to feel the force of it. The wrecking ball has already demolished the building, you see. I'm just sifting through the debris to see if there's anything worth saving."

"And?" I piped.

"You'll have to read the book. Although frankly I very much doubt if I'll ever finish it. Actually I don't want to finish it. It's a place to dwell, a place where I can have a symposium with myself. Sounds crazy, I know, but I think you, Donald especially, may know what I mean. But where did it begin, this soul sickness? The Depression? World War II? No, I think earlier and maybe much earlier. And it's not just America, you see. It's the same in Europe, this ennui, this jaded quality combined with existential despair. We're like rats that are desperate to leave a sinking ship, but there's nowhere to go because the ship is the world and the doors of the world are barred and locked and sealed. Some theorists think it all began with the Industrial Revolution. James Watt invents the steam engine, the potato arrives in England from Peru, and suddenly there's an abundance of food, which leads to a population explosion and a movement away from the land and into the cities as peasants leave off farming and go to work in Blake's dark satanic mills."

The Professor refilled our glasses with absinthe-green Chartreuse. "But if we zoom out still further we can say that the development of agriculture ten thousand years ago in the Fertile Crescent was itself the beginning of a disastrous culture shift. The freedom of the hunter gatherer lifestyle, our connection with the natural world, passed away, and as mystery faded, the birth of the written word—the development of the phonetic alphabet—gradually weaned our consciousness away from the old world of gestalt pictographic awareness and into the abstract world of written language, into what I would call the tyranny of the mind."

"This is the germ, then, of our demise, of *Der Untergang Des Abendlandes?*" Roderick interjected.

"I don't know. I can't say for sure. I'm still searching for it. What I do know is that Spengler pole-axed this civilization; he knocked it ass over teakettle and left us with a stinking corpse. We're the survivors, the fellaheen, the spiritually gelded men who march like wooden soldiers to our jobs, to the polls, to the stadium, to the bar, always with the stink of purification in our nostrils. But almost certainly there was a time in the distant past when we were right with ourselves. After all, the human race began some 250,000 years ago in Africa, but the bloody and brutal story of recorded history covers only the last five thousand years. There have been other civilizations, you see. Archaeologists are uncovering new layers every day. What we call recorded history is just the tip of an iceberg. The point is, somewhere along the line the human race missed an onramp, or perhaps I should say an offramp. The Golden Age isn't a myth. It's a racial memory that's just now emerging from the Collective Unconscious. This 21st century malaise is at the bottom nostalgia—nostalgia for the freedom and for a magical sense of connectedness we once knew. We need to make a U-turn, go back and turn around, retrace our steps, go back and recover our lost wholeness. *Down, not up!* This is what I want to shout from the housetops. It's no good sending rockets to Jupiter and Mars. We have to dig deeper. We have to go back, back to the Neolithic, back to the Paleolithic World Order. This is where the clues will be found. Not in the sky."

Our glasses were now empty, but Professor Van Rysselberge had a surprise for us: a bottle of *Élixir Végétal de la Grande-Chartreuse*, brewed, he explained by the same monks who make the ordinary garden variety Chartreuse we'd been drinking. "142 proof," he intoned. "Distilled from more than 130 aromatic and medicinal herbs, plants and flowers...some of which must almost certainly be... psychotropic."

Since Élixir Végétal was completely new to me, and even, I gathered, to Roderick, the Professor showed us how one drinks this magical potion. Three small glasses, a sugar cube in each, add a shot of Perrier, stir lightly. Now add just a few tiny drops of Élixir Végétal to each glass, stir once again, very lightly, let it fizz for a moment or two, and bottoms up, lads. We clinked glasses, nodded bravely at each other, and—wham! An instant later I was in palookaville, pleasantly palookaville, okay, sure, even euphorically palookaville, but I also knew that I'd been hit with a left hook that I never saw coming.

I remember Roderick helping me up the stairs to my room, and then he was tucking me in, and I was looking up at his cheery bearded face, and I couldn't stop laughing. Edward Lear's lines from *The Book of Nonsense* were going through my head, "Two owls and a hen, four larks and a wren, have all built nests in my beard," And I swear I really did see the sweetest little birds flittering and twittering in Roderick's long gray beard. "Four larks and a wren," I babbled. "Four larks and a wren! Right? Edward Lear, right? Don't let me forget. Write it down, okay? Please! It's important!"

Sleep was claiming me. I was falling into the heart of a carnivorous flower. It was all nonsense, wasn't it? Books, writing? Nonsense, deadwood, gobbledygook. The book the Professor was writing, the book I was writing, even Spengler, even *Der Untergang Des Abendlandes*...

"Roderick, do you remember the cats?" I managed.

"The cats. Ha ha! Sure, I remember the cats."

"The one with the white paw..."

"Yes...yes. Those were the days."

"And the black one."

"Sure, I remember. I loved those cats."

"I know..."

11

*I*n one of Fausto's unpublished literary novels—a real book, not the Fernando de León schlock he cranks out by the yard for Norma Jacoby and Ruby Fine—a hobo riding in a boxcar dreams of a simpler way of life. A new world unfolds in his mind. He sees himself walking through lush green meadows where laughing children dance and play. From the top of a hill he watches America's great cities empty as enthusiasm for work declines. The people begin farming the land, the grazing animals return, and the wolves, and the old ways come back. "I remember now," the hobo murmurs in his sleep. "You catch it and you eat it, and you leave the bones and move on."

That was Fausto, the real Fausto, the Fausto I'd known back in the early days, the Suzy Soojian days, before this ennui, this 21st century soul syphilis came over him. Fausto the holy primitive, Fausto the natural man. Simple, lusty, unadorned. Leave the bones and move on. But now...

We went to La Pachanga for a few *pistos* and to hash things over. It had been a while. Fausto was in an awful state. The *hombre de papel* business again, and how he's lost his soul and all that, but now there was a new development, stemming from an incident two nights ago at the Kona Kai Club, the Barefoot Bar. He was a little drunk but minding his own business, and pretty soon a bevy of French tourist girls plunked themselves down at his table. Everybody was slurping up Mai Tais and before long one of the French cuties starts playing footsie with him under the table. Of course! That's Fausto. The old Fernando de León floy floy, it never fails. He doesn't have to *do* anything. *Pheromones.* The man emits pheromones like a cabbage moth. So they're playing footsie and he sticks his bare foot up under her skirt and it turns out she wasn't wearing any pants. "French girls don't, you know," he confides slyly. So he pokes the big toe of his left foot inside her and begins working it around.

"How did she..."

"How did she like it? My god, man, she went ballistic! You should have heard the shriek she let out when she got her gun. Everybody was staring at us. You'd think an air raid siren went off. I thought she'd dissolve my fucking toe, she was so juiced up. The syrup was pouring out of her like molten lava. She opened up like an artichoke. I could easily have gotten my whole foot in there. It was like stepping in quicksand. I thought she was going to suck me right into herself. You know, it might seem strange, but actually you can feel a lot more with your toe than you can with your prick. Did you know that? All the little layers, so squirmy, like a ball of worms. The tunnel of love, man. The tunnel of love... After that she was mad for me. Wouldn't leave me alone. She followed me around like a dog in heat, even barged right into the men's room. I couldn't take a piss without her grabbing for my cock..."

The rest was hazy as he'd really been belting them down. They went up to his room and he gave her the time and then the two of them conked out. It had been a perfect evening for Fausto but apparently not so for mademoiselle, because a couple hours later he woke up, dazed, and here she was sitting in a chair by the bed, masturbating, with "...the most agonized look on her face. Jesus, Donaldo, that's the part I can't get over. *Her expression*..." She was diddling herself off and she couldn't get it, couldn't get it, and finally she sees Fausto sitting up in bed staring at her and she says, "*Cherie*, could you please do it again...like before, *avec le gros ortiel*—with your big toe?" And that did it. Fausto was destroyed.

I burst out laughing, but Fausto couldn't be jollied out of his desolate mood. "Do you see what this means, man?" he wailed. "She liked my big toe better than my dick. It's *humiliating!*"

I bought us a round of beers and tried to change the subject, but nothing doing. Fausto was just getting warmed up. "I hustled her out of there, man. Sent her packing. I never had a woman insult me like that before. Then I took a good look at myself in the mirror. I'm forty-three years old, man! I'm losing my hair and that's not the worst of it. Did you know that your penis gets smaller as you get older? It's true. I saw it on the Internet. You lose a fraction of an inch each year. Your spine settles too. Something to do with the vertebrae. The discs dry out and collapse, or some shit like that. It's wicked! The cartilage wears away, and you get progressively shorter and shorter. It's a medical fact. I used to be six feet tall, man! Now I'm probably only about five-eight. Go ahead and laugh if you want to. You're no spring chicken, you know. You think none of this bullshit is going to touch you, but you're wrong. The clock is ticking, brother. Every hour, every minute, every second, your dick is getting smaller. It's a fact of life."

"What was her name?" I ventured.

"Who? What was whose name?"

"The French girl."

"Name? I never ask their names. Simone, maybe. She didn't have a name. Mademoiselle from Armentieres, for all I care. The cunt!"

I should have known. Fausto's women never had

names. Women to Fausto were a commodity, agents for his penis, nothing more. He'd refer to them, when he'd regale me for hours with tales of his conquests, as "the one with the big tits," or "the one with the little pink mole on her ass," or "the one who sucked me off at Sardi's," etc. Pursuing this scenario, the French girl at the Kona Kai would undoubtedly become, "the one I fucked with my big toe."

Another round and the alcohol is starting to kick in. He's becoming philosophical. "You know, what I liked about that French cutie in the first place was the armpit hair. That was what turned me on more than anything. French girls don't shave under their arms. But you know that. You lived in Paris, right? When you see that hair under their arms it's a huge turn-on, at least for me. It's the excitement of the chase, I guess, like when the hounds first get the scent of the fox. It's almost as they've got an *auxiliary* pussy tucked away in their armpit. I mean that's what it reminds you of. Or you might say that it's sort of a preview of their regular pussy. That's why I want to get back to Europe where women don't fucking shave their armpits every five minutes. I mean, this is bullshit over here. If I had my life to live over again, you know what I'd do? I'd measure my dick when I was twenty-five, then again at thirty and again at forty. Keep a record of it, you know? Nice and neat, maybe in one of those little ledgers like Swiss bankers carry in their vest pocket. That way you could tell how much you were losing each year, or even month by month."

He's finally calming down, but now there's something else he has to tell me about. He's decided to quit writing—for good. At first I thought he was joking, but no, he's dead serious. The Rimbaud Option, he calls it. He made the decision a month ago, in fact. But he's been backsliding, and he wants my help.

We decide to leave La Pachanga and head over to the Wilshire Royal Hotel bar, my old haunt. As we're walking through Lafayette Park he explains to me what he means by the Rimbaud Option.

"Sure, I admit it sounds crazy, I mean a guy like me deciding to quit writing and live a normal life. I mean, it's like John Dillinger becoming a Buddhist monk. Or like the Pope suddenly announcing to the world that he's planning to marry a Jew. But let's face it, Donaldo. We're never going to get published. So instead of plodding on and on, adding one line to another, cranking out paragraphs, words, manuscripts—instead of jacking off out the window, in other words—just do one thing. *Abdicate*. Walk out, quit, serve notice! *Jeanne Nicolas Arthur Rimbaud*. What a story, what a life! At age twenty-one Rimbaud quits writing and dives headfirst into the life of the world. He goes to Africa and becomes a diamond merchant and a gunrunner—even a slave trader. Rimbaud turned his back on literature. He abdicated his role as a poet. Now we have to do the same. We've got to say, fuck it, man, I'm over it. But..."

"But what?"

"It's not easy."

It's not easy because there's still a tiny flickering flame in Fausto. Fausto's dead, the paper man is dead, the *hombre de papel*, but he's not dead enough. He can't stop writing. *The voices...*

"My friend, I once believed that it was my mission on earth to inject magic and mystery into the dead superstructure of the world, a skeleton divested of flesh. The problem is, I still believe it. The inner child is a tyrant, my friend."

"Don't you think I know that?"

At the Wilshire Royale I found myself sitting at the bar next to a tourist lady who was nursing a bourbon old fashioned with three cherries and two orange slices— Marlena's drink— and I thought, my God, how much time has gone by? That plump, gray-haired over-rouged tourist lady could actually *be* Marlena and I wouldn't even recognize her—and in that moment I realized with a jolt what Fausto was getting at about the passage of time and pissing out a window and all.

"Wake up and smell the coffee, my friend," Fausto was saying. "You're not getting any younger, you know. You need to marry Doreen and settle down, that's what you need to do. Get a regular job, live a normal life! Look, I know it's hard to believe that I'd ever be saying something like this after all we've been through, but shit, man, there comes a time. And you two were made for each other, everybody says so. Weren't you ghostwriting her memoirs at one point? *The Oomph Girl,* wasn't it? You know, she's one crazy chick. That's why she's right for you. You're both crazy. I mean in a good way. Well, you know what I mean. Listen, Donaldo, how long do you think she's going to put up with that putz, a fucking used car salesman from Bellflower? Doreen's an intelligent woman, a cultured woman. Let her have her fling, get it out of her system. She'll be back, I guarantee it."

He orders a round of Cuba Libres and gives me the bottom line: he wants to renew his pledge to quit writing and he wants me to join him. He wants me to take the pledge too—the Rimbaud Option—right here and now, at the historic Wilshire Hotel bar, and he wants to shake on it, a blood oath, like the Knights of the Roundtable, the blood brothers sort of thing, with no bullshit and no backing down.

"So far, I admit, Donaldo, my Flight to Tarshish has been a failure. I vowed to quit writing, but now I find myself listening once again to the fucking *voices,* those demonic, tyrannical voices that dictate to me day and night. Implicit in their torrential outpouring is the mandate, which I now find impossible to disobey: *whatever I say, you will write down.* You see? How to crush the demon of creativity! This is the problem I'm wrestling with now, my friend. I'm more than willing to give General Grant my sword. But I can't stop writing! This desire for an ending...it could be the desire for death, the desire to flow back into the buttonmold, but it could also be seen as a wish for the annihilation of the ego. I admit that I don't know how to crush the demon of creativity. I don't know how to exorcise the demon. I am in essence that demon. How to kill the inner child, that's what it comes down to. *How to kill the inner child.* I want to live a normal life. But how can one live a normal life in Los Angeles?"

A few days later I had a visit from Cliff English. I don't know how he found me. He was appalled of course at my digs, the piles of junk, the ticking refrigerator, the mad sculptor puttering with his radios. Cliff was affable enough, but I knew he'd been sent by Norma Jacoby to reconnoiter, to find out where I was living, etc, so I was secretly pleased when he tried to pet the orange tabby and got a nice set of bloody furrows on his left forearm for his trouble.

As luck would have it, Schvedchikov had mopped the bathroom floor just minutes before Cliff arrived, and the disinfectant made Cliff's eyes water so furiously that he suggested we repair to La Pachanga for beers. As we were settling in, Cliff mentioned that he'd heard through the grapevine that Fausto had taken a job as a security guard at a movie set, and I felt sheepish about that because although I'd shaken hands with my old pal and sworn a blood oath earlier that week at the Wilshire Royale when the two of us had solemnly pledged to quit writing forever and lead normal lives, I had neither stopped scribbling nor looked for work. I'd been going over in my mind the encounter at the bar with Marlena's double, and I was becoming obsessed with the idea that the lady with the bourbon old fashioned and the three cherries was a karmic apparition, and I desperately wanted to confront Fausto, or even the bartender, and ask him, *did you see her too?* Then there was the thing about Grobbel. Ever since that day in the park with Tom and Marge and Mad Rosa when

Donald O'Donovan

Roderick told Grobbel's story about the Freakmaker, I'd been wondering about Grobbel, that is, was there really a Grobbel, or was Grobbel, as I suspected, someone Roderick had made up and was the tale about the hunchback actually his, Roderick's story? And now, as I began thinking once again about Marlena and the life we shared, old memories returned and I found myself once again in Paris, broke and alone, stumbling into a sea of umbrellas and *pointilliste* raindrops shimmering on Boulevard Saint Germain in front of Brasserie Lipp, and it seemed to me in that moment that somehow *I* was Grobbel, the scarecrow who sleeps on the Metro. *How could she have been so heartless? How could she have abandoned me?* But an even more excruciating possibility was gestating in my mind: that the dumpy grayhaired woman at the bar of the Wilshire Royale Hotel *actually was* Marlena, and she had been "sent" there to tell me: "See, this is what happens to our great loves. They get old and fat and wrinkled and bockle-faced, and so do you, and time is flying, little man, and Fausto is right, your life is slipping away, minute by minute, and you'd better dip your bread in the gravy while it's still hot."

The following day I caught a bus over to Hollywood to pick up my mail at general delivery, bills and a postcard from Starz. I tossed the bills in the trash without opening them and stuck the postcard in my pocket. I was still thinking about Marlena and I was going over the karmic apparition business in my mind as well, and I thought a stroll on Hollywood Boulevard might prove lenitive, mentally speaking. I was thinking too about Peg Entwistle and her fatal dive off the Hollywood Sign.

A few blocks later as I was standing at the corner of Hollywood and Vine waiting for a light and watching a gorgeous street-stepper defiantly flirting with two plainclothes cops, I absent-mindedly fished Starz's postcard out of my pocket. The card from Starz was postmarked Iquitos Peru. "Could be getting some great

110

footage if I had a camera." Same old Starz. At least he was out of the lunatic asylum. Sold his camera to a Portuguese riverboat captain for drinking money, he said. Yep, same old Starz. Or was he? Starz had never sold his camera before, not even on his colossal binges in Las Vegas or his super colossals in Marrakech and Kuala Lumpur.

I felt something settling on me, a black cloud. At first I thought it was just Hollywood Boulevard bringing me down, and then I thought it might be Marlena or even Peg Entwistle—so young, so gifted, so doomed—a Valkyrie brought down by the pom-pom guns. But finally I realized that it was the camera that got me. He'd never sold his camera before, he'd never done that. Starz was sinking below the horizon, I knew it, I could feel it. And that thought so depressed me that when I got back to my cell with the brown cheesecloth curtains brittle as old sheets of newsprint and the wobbly table and my rickety chair, my lopsided bunk with the three patched army blankets and down the hall the ancient refrigerator that ticked like a time bomb, I kicked a crumpled-up beer can across the room and I said to myself, "You know what? Fuck this shit! I'm going to get a job, get married and live a normal life." It was too late for Starz, but maybe not for me. I could still get married again. Sure, there was still time. And I'd show Fausto that I was dead serious about the Rimbaud Option. In 1875 Rimbaud wrote "Dawn is a people of doves" on the wall of the Hotel de Ville and he abdicated, he turned his back on the bastards. Rimbaud was right and Fausto was right. "Shit, I can do normal," I said aloud in a firm voice. "You want normal? I'll show you normal. I'll pay taxes, I'll watch the ballgame, I'll even fucking wear pajamas and eat a soft boiled egg on toast in my bathrobe while I'm reading the morning paper; I'll mow the lawn in my shirtsleeves and play catch with the kid, and me and the little woman by God we'll have it all, the Chevy Nova, the Jack Russell terrier and the pink plastic lawn flamingoes."

The next morning I left the sculptor's lair bright and early and began pounding the pavement. Around noon I stopped into the Paradise Lounge to use the toilet, and a program came on TV, "The Ten Keys to Success." I don't remember the other nine keys, but the first one was: *Take stock of yourself. What are your abilities? What are your skills? What do you want to do with your life? What do you desire from the world?*

I sat down at the bar, ordered a gin straight up, and tried to assess my situation with ice-cold logic. What do I desire from the world? What do I want to do with my life? What are my skills? I was passably well schooled in a number of métiers. I knew how to drive a truck, flip a burger, stuff a corpse, pound a nail, teach a class, deliver a newspaper, make a donut, repair a shoe, bounce a drunk, fix a roller skate, dig a hole, frame a wall, figure an estimate, pump a toilet and plenty more.

Someone had left the *Los Angeles Times* on the bar, and in the classifieds I spied an ad: "Telephone sales, start today!" I caught a bus to the address, a boiler room on Sixth a block east of Broadway. It was two flights up over the Club Savoy, a taxi-dance joint where I'd spent many desperate hours trying to pry my way into the stiff taffeta evening dresses of the iron maidens who charged $1.95 a minute for a whirl around the dance floor.

I'm shitting my pants with nervousness, but the guy hires me on the spot. He shows me to my desk. The product was encyclopedias. You got a minimum hourly wage plus a commission on leads. So far so good. He hands me a copy of the canned speech I'm supposed to deliver. After five calls I knew the patter by heart.

Next to me sat a guy named Eldridge Pribble. At precisely two o'clock each afternoon this Pribble would take out of his desk drawer some tortilla chips wrapped in a brown paper napkin. I think it's even possible that there was a certain number of chips that never varied. After glancing cautiously around and sniffing the air, he'd delicately pick up a single chip and nibble around the circumference of it. You could hear him munching, munching, like a chipmunk. Then he'd pop the chip, much reduced in size, into his mouth. When the chip became moderately soggy he'd crush it against the roof of his mouth with his tongue, meanwhile reaching for a second chip. There's a distinct difference between the sound produced by a tongue crushing a crisp tortilla chip and by a tongue crushing a soggy tortilla chip against the roof of one's mouth.

After a week of this insanity I walked out of the office and never went back. I didn't even bother to collect the few dollars that were coming to me. What ever led me to believe that I could sell encyclopedias? It's a mystery to me today. I hadn't developed any leads. I'd actually made very few calls. Instead, I'd daydreamed the time away. Instead of making calls I'd made notes for an essay—on order forms, on bar receipts, envelopes, anything I could grab. It was frantic. I was sure I was onto something. My head was bursting. The words were shooting out of my fingertips. *Knowledge is death.* That was the thesis of my essay. Why encyclopedias? That was the underlying idea. Why sell encyclopedias? Why compile them? Why print them? Why print more encyclopedias, and more and more? Why go on pretending that knowledge is the key? Why indulge in more and more of this chipmunk chatter? Why bite around the edges of the problem, why swallow another mouthful?

When I closed my eyes I saw the Pribbles of the world—the emerging Chipmunk Men of the Information Age—nibbling at the dead corpus of knowledge with a fervor that belied their unconscious recognition of the death that was already on them. Because today the real desire, our deepest desire, and the unspoken prayer on lips of every human being is: "*God, make me a healthy animal.*"

To kill without remorse, to gorge to the full, to sleep in the sunshine, to die without regret—this is what I desire from the world.

12

I got a letter from Hugo van der Weyden. The mauve stationery, the West Palm Beach postmark. I put the unopened letter down somewhere and promptly forgot about it. Later I remembered and searched my room but I couldn't turn it up, a shame because I always enjoyed Hugo's letters, not only because he was one of my few correspondents who hadn't switched to email, but also because Hugo was something of a litterateur and he liked to reminisce about the old days in Paris. Then a few days later at a laundromat as I was stuffing my dirty clothes in the washer I found the letter in a shirt pocket. While the machine was doing its thing I plunked myself down on a bench, opened the letter, and out fell a check—a check for one...thousand...dollars. In a daze I read the brief note:

"Donaldo, my friend. Please accept this vote of confidence from an old pal. I know you can use it because the world is never kind to your sort of person. I believe in you. You've always been an inspiration to me."

I immediately burst into tears, and I must have made quite a commotion, because pretty soon a lady in a fur coat came up to me and gave me a five-dollar bill along with a slip of paper on which she'd written the address of a homeless shelter. And before I could protest or explain she'd squeezed my hand and sailed out the door, all without a word. I realized that of course she thought I was homeless when she saw my torn shirt and ill-fitting pants. I'd dressed that morning in my oldest goodwill store clothes so I could put my newest goodwill store clothes in the laundry. It was too late to chase after the lady and give her back the five bucks, and besides, I'd made up my mind to accept that five-dollar bill as a second vote of confidence, on top of Hugo's vote of confidence. It was all coming together now, the pledge I'd made to Fausto, the check from Hugo, the kind lady in the fur coat who squeezed my hand and gave me five dollars. This was a vote of confidence from the universe. It was redemption, it was absolution. I was being handed a new life. Through the window of the washer I could see my clothes whirling in the sudsy water. That was *me* in there, spinning merrily around, and those soap suds were washing away the past— the sordidness, the defeats, the despair. It was a baptism. I was being baptized, cleansed, renewed, and after the rinse and spin cycles I would emerge spanking clean, a new man.

I wish I could tell you that the minute I'd cashed Hugo's check I packed a suitcase and made a beeline for the Fairfax district and that sunny garret room with the nice Jewish lady, but the truth is I stuffed the money in my pocket and made a beeline for the Las Palmas Dancehall to look for the Russian girl my pal Starz had stolen from me all those months ago in Malibu, but damned if I could remember her name. Sofia? Regina? Marina? While waiting for a taxi in front of Bullock's Wilshire with that huge wad of bills burning a hole in my pocket, I tried my best to remember. Renata? Dominika? At the same time an adage I'd heard since I was a kid was going through my mind, "If you don't treat yourself well, how can you expect others to treat you well?" I was plenty sold on this bit of folk wisdom and I fully intended to treat myself well, and then some. What I had in mind was a nice bottle of champagne, a great meal, and a woman, preferably in that order. A taxi pulled up and I got in, and all the way across town I tried to remember. Valentina? Anastasia? Nothing sounded quite right. Then, after we made the elbow turn at 7th and I saw the strutting pigeons clustered at the foot of the Sanwa Plaza angel sculpture her name finally popped into my head: *Svetlana!*

Svetlana was the dime-a-dance queen of the Las Palmas Dancehall; she was everybody's angel, and those pigeons were the dancehall Romeos who clustered around her, strutting and flaunting their feathers, old geezers with fakey toupees and dyed eyebrows and pencil-thin mustaches they'd trimmed in lonely rooms with rusty manicure scissors, characters you'd expect to see in a Bogart movie. Some of these bozos, no exaggeration, were pushing ninety. A stiff breeze would have bowled them over. You'd think by God that a man could have some peace in his declining years from the demands of the sex demon, but no, a trickle of testosterone was still flowing in these ancient relics, so out they'd go of an evening, all snazzed up, reeking of cheap cologne, slickum on their hair, looking for some trim. No quiet evenings at home for these old farts! They'd hide their canes outside the door, some of them. I swear I'm not exaggerating. It was pathetic. And in between dances they'd crowd around Svetlana, the lot of them, exactly like those puffed-up pigeons at Sanwa Plaza, strutting and preening and cooing, "Choose me! Choose me!"

There were young guys too of course, twenty year-old kids with jail tattoos, sinister cholos from east LA, fierce Tongans, bulky as sumo wrestlers, and zenlike oriental dudes with wispy goatees who looked like they could fell an ironwood tree with a single karate chop—even tourists from Des Moines and Cleveland who'd blundered into the place thinking it was a whorehouse. They weren't far from wrong, either, because bling is the thing when it comes to the ladies, at least at the Las Palmas Dancehall, and tonight, by Jesus, I had it in spades. *Money talks and bullshit walks, gentlemen.* There's nothing like a few crisp Benjamins to cool the action and seal a deal. I knew the minute I stepped inside the place that I'd be leaving with Svetlana, I was that sure of myself. The bidding is closed, gentlemen. You can lope your mules tonight. I'm in the catbird seat this time around, and no mistake about it.

I can't tell you how goddamn good it felt to get into a taxi with a smashing girl and tell the driver, "Westin Bonaventure." Living well is the best revenge, as someone or other once said. Svetlana was tickled pink, of course, about the hotel. That and the Dom Pérignon and the room service Lobster Newburg. I think that's why she came through with something more than a pleasant show of enthusiasm. I thought she was going to bounce me right off the ceiling, as a matter of fact. Not that I wouldn't have settled for a pleasant show of enthusiasm. It's better not to expect too much from the world, I find. Champagne is wonderful, but you don't walk around your whole life with your mouth full of champagne. It's the same with women. You get the barnacles scraped off your prow and you weigh anchor. So long!

On the morning of the third day I sent Svetlana home in a taxi. I wanted to be alone. Being alone isn't half bad when you've got money. I sat by the pool, soaking up the ambiance, thinking about the women I've known. You remember their faces, their breasts...no, not even that. Their scent, maybe, or perhaps just bits and pieces of conversation. But Svetlana, what a woman. How could I have forgotten her name? Must remember to tell Fausto, incidentally, that Russian girls don't shave their armpits. I'm wondering now what ever became of Vanessa from Azusa? Or Doreen for that matter? Or Marlena? And was Marlena my second wife or my third wife? I can't remember, it seems so long ago. Or maybe they're just karmic apparitions, these women. But Vanessa... My childhood crush was named Vanessa. She lived across the street. We'd sail paper boats in mud puddles when the snow melted. Funny how little it takes to make you happy when you're young and innocent. Later on it takes more, a lot more. Women, booze, drugs. The annihilation of the ego, even. But being young isn't all it's cracked up to be. I just wish Fausto could understand that. No sooner are you out of diapers than they pack you off to war. Or else you go from a troubled adolescence right into midlife crisis and from there straight into senile dementia without a break anywhere along the line. You think I'm kidding? I know people... But I agree with Fausto about the armpit hair business. When it comes to a woman I want something fresh from the veldt, not processed cheese. Speaking of processed cheese, I've been trying to remember my first wife's name. Eleanor? Elvira? I suppose it doesn't matter. Does anything matter? Equanimity is the word that's coming to the fore. The annihilation of the ego, sure, but bliss is not the goal. Bliss is for teenagers. *Equanimity*. It doesn't matter. Equanimity is the Tao. Edwina? Amanda? Gwendolyn? Nope, none of the above. The names fall away too, one finds. Karmic apparitions

...If you don't escape from the wheel of birth and death this time around you could come back as a cockroach, so they say. Or a dog. Dogs have it made, at least in America. Not so in Mexico where starving scavenger dogs haunt the streets like hyenas. In Vietnam it's worse. If you're a dog in Vietnam they'll eat you. So it's probably better not to be born a dog in Vietnam.

A waiter is hurrying with umbrella drinks, a sparrow is pecking at a crumb near my foot, the swaying palms are sweeping puffy white clouds away from the horizon. I'm remembering last night, the Dom Pérignon—those tiny bubbles! And the Lobster Newburg. And Svetlana. Svetlana, what a woman! She'll scrape the barnacles off your prow. Money's a wonderful thing. I still have a few Benjamins left. I can order an umbrella drink if I like. Can call a taxi, can order a meal. Could even rent that sunny garret room in the Fairfax district with the nice Jewish lady. It's still a possibility if I don't piss the rest of the money away. She'd bring me a warm strawberry knish in the morning, I know she would. She'd probably give me a bath, too. I mean if I was a dog. That'd be something, wouldn't it? *Bow-wow-wow!* That'd be beautiful. Yes! I could get used to that shit...

13

*L*ife at Bill's goat farm in Reseda was great. I learned the difference between hay and straw, between a boar and a sow, a foal and a mare, a colt and a filly, and between pasture and tillage, and I picked up a beautiful word, "tilth," a loamy, nutrient-rich, organic word straight out of Middle English that surely must have been one of Chaucer's favorite words. There were four of us workers, Dolly and Delia, sisters, BirutÄ— from Belgium and me. We were charged with the care and feeding of 150 Nubian goats. Dolly with the gold-flecked eyes had done a flushable tampon commercial, her sister Delia was trying to write a romance novel, and BirutÄ— from Belgium had played Desdemona in summer theater. It was beautiful out there in the country and I adored the Goat Girls.

Looking back, the business about the sunny garret room with the nice Jewish lady, that was just a fantasy, but the goat farm was real. Bill's wife Frieda served huge farm breakfasts at 4am in the spacious dimly-lit kitchen. It was pitch black outside when we fell to—scrambled eggs, ham, bacon—sometimes even steak—and hash browns and homemade biscuits with sausage gravy, and waffles with real maple syrup.

Bill was short, muscular and painfully sunburned. He smelled like stale sweat and animal dung.

"You can't pitch hay on Rice Krispies!" he told us.

Bill would be out in the fields all morning, haying, and later, around ten or eleven, Frieda would climb up in a tractor and take his lunch out to him. The Goat Girls and I ate our meals in the barn sitting on bales of hay. Outside in the barnyard you'd see frantic chickens pecking and clucking and baby goats pronking and the little girls in their summer dresses—Bill and Frieda's children—would be having a tea party underneath the eucalyptus trees or swinging merrily on the rope swing.

When my mates at the goat farm found out that I was a writer they were unduly impressed. *You, a writer?* Immediately they christened me "Shakespeare Junior." It didn't matter to them that I was a paperback writer, a pornographer, that the books I'd published were the purest schlock, the veriest horse shit. I was a writer, a *published* writer, an author. That was all that mattered. Dolly, even that golden-eyed lioness of a flushable tampon Dolly, she came up to me: "I'd like to talk to you about *literature*."

I was mortified. "Oh, Jesus," I said. "I don't care anything about that."

"Yes, you do. Who're your favorite authors? Stephen King? Hemingway? Faulkner? Come on, tell me."

"Well—William Blake."

"William Blake? Sure, I know William Blake. Isn't he the guy that translated James Joyce into English?"

It was right after this that I had a dream in which I was Shakespeare himself. And since it was decided that I was quitting writing for forever I had the unenviable task of discharging my Muse. Sitting in the empty Globe Theater scribbling on thick scratchy paper with a quill pen, I was feeling somewhat nervous and also desperately sad, but I figured that by pretending to be working on one of my novels I might be able to summon the dear Lady and then

I'd give her the bad news. But when she showed up I was astonished that instead of an old Irish washerwoman with a mouthful of clothespins gabbing to me over a back fence as I'd always envisioned, my Muse was actually a soulful Joan Baez *La Belle Dame Sans Merci* dryad who cantered out of a midsummer night's dream on a white unicorn, attended by peacocks and elves, and in that moment I realized that I was going to have a devil of a job giving such a glorious creature her walking papers. But fortunately at this juncture I woke up...

Shakespeare Junior! It was as if I were made out of gold. Nothing was too good for me after that. I didn't have to shovel shit, for example. And the girls would bring me coffee in the morning. But the goat farm gig paid only for room and board, and if I was going to become a normal person and live a sensible life I had to make some paper, so I got myself a job three days a week at Stanton's Market in Reseda where the Valley's Beautiful People shopped.

I worked with Mickey Gilhooley, a dedicated drunk. We were both from New York, so we had that in common, but Mickey had lived in Reseda for fifteen years, harking back—as he never tired of mentioning—to the big Northridge quake in '94, and since Reseda was squatting right on top of the San Andreas Fault, in my mind it was almost as if the Earth herself had burped Mickey Gilhooley up.

Our day began at 8am. We'd put up the orders and get ready to go to people's houses. Valley folks had their groceries delivered. When we'd head out to the delivery van, around 10am, Mickey would already be four sheets to the wind and aggressively friendly. He'd buttonhole you, blowing his whiskey breath in your face, his speech slurred and garbled, and he'd tell you stories about the time he worked on the Erie Canal, and then he'd burst into song:

"Where do you work a-John
on the Delaware Lawawann
A-wann, a-wann, a-wann!"

Then he'd laugh uproariously and pound you on the back, as though it were the greatest joke in the world. You were so close to him now that you could see the individual breadcrumbs trapped in his ratty reddish mustache and the blotchy network of red and purple spider veins that gave his cheeks an eerie alcoholic glow. With his watery blue eyes swimming in his red burgher's face, his tie pulled to one side, and his vest halfway buttoned over his little potbelly, he looked like a jaded elf or a pregnant leprechaun.

Once we got rolling it wasn't so bad. The pace was leisurely, and we'd frequently stop by Mickey's digs on Cantara so he could fix, or else he'd bring a bottle with him, usually a quart of Rittenhouse Monongahela Rye. Around noon or 1pm we'd park at the Duck Pond on Victory Boulevard and eat hero sandwiches we'd bought at Stanton's Market with our employee discount.

Mrs. Tingley, on Runnymeade, was a regular customer. Buxomy, flirty, a little shopworn, and she was pretty heavily into the sauce. She lived with her moms, and often when we'd arrive with their groceries the two of them would be sitting at the white plastic table in the kitchen, lushing it up, and Moms would get out her "Best of Roy Rogers" album and play *San Fernando Valley* for us.

"I really love Roy Rogers," Moms would often say, "but I do think Bing Crosby does a better job than Roy on *San Fernando Valley*. I mean, Bing's got style."

One afternoon in June we went to the house on Runnymeade. Mrs. Tingley was in mourning for her daughter, Patsy, who'd been killed in a car wreck on high school graduation night just days before. We rang the bell and Mrs. Tingley received us, rather gushingly, I thought. I smelled wine on her breath. The two top buttons of her blouse were open and I looked down her bra. Her perfume made my head reel.

"Mickey, would you like a drink? How about you,

er...David, is it?"

"Donald, ma'am. No thank you, ma'am."

While Mickey was slurping it down, I followed Mrs. Tingley into the kitchen where Moms, I noticed, was passed out at the white plastic table, with a snapshot at her elbow of Patsy standing in front of the old Reseda Theater.

"You'll have to excuse my mother," Mrs. Tingley said. "She's had a bit too much to drink." I followed Mrs. Tingley into the pantry. "I want you to look at my flour bin," she said. "I'm afraid it's bugs. But it could be mice. I'd just like you to take a look."

This, as if I were an expert in such matters.

She flipped open the plastic lid of the flour bin and leaned over to peer inside, at the same time unbuttoning another button on her blouse. My heart did a flip-flop. Mrs. Tingley's nipples were brown, just like her eyes.

"Look at these little black things. I think it must be a mouse. What do you think, Donald?"

"I think you've got a mouse, Mrs. Tingley."

"Oh, God. I've always been afraid of those things. By the way, I wish you would call me Pamela. You know, I wish I'd never left Thousand Oaks. We never had mice in T.O. Mice are so...so... I mean, you feel like they could run right up you, those furry little creatures. If you're a woman, I mean. They're *icky!*"

We were standing close together. My dick was twitching madly inside my pants. Mrs. Tingley glanced up at the clock on the wall. "Two-thirty. Patsy would have been at cheerleading practice right now," she murmured, "If she had lived, I mean." She took out a hanky and dabbed at her eyes.

"I'm sorry, Mrs. Tingley."

"Call me Pamela, please."

"Pamela..."

I got my courage up and touched her breast. She dropped her hand down between us and brushed my bursting fly with her knuckles. The whole exchange took place with such hallucinating swiftness that I wasn't sure if it was a masturbation fantasy produced by my febrile mind or if it actually happened.

"I don't want something like that to crawl up me. Do you know what I mean, Donald?"

"Of course..."

"I want to show you a photo of Patsy," she whispered intently, as if it were the most important thing in the world. She grasped my shoulders and pressed down, planting me to the spot. Then she darted back into the kitchen and returned with a gilt-framed photo of Patsy in her white cheerleader's sweater.

"This was from when we lived in T.O.," she said.

"She was a beautiful girl."

"Do you think I look like her?" Mrs. Tingley murmured, breathing warmly in my face, her lips very close to mine.

"Very much," I intoned, "*Especially*..." I slipped my hand inside her bra and gently pinched her nipple. I felt her hand brush my fly again.

"You mean the *breasts*?"

She pointed, on the photo, at Patsy's hooters. She had her hand on me now, and I was working my knee around in her crotch. It was as if we were masturbating together to her daughter's photo.

"Yes, Pamela..."

"Do you like my breasts?"

"Yes, Pamela..."

"Better than Patsy's?"

"Yes, Pamela..." I had both of her tits out now, and I was kissing them. We headed for her bedroom, with her clutching Patsy's photo. In the kitchen we encountered Mickey, who was pouring himself a stiff one. I made some excuse and we dived into Mrs. Tingley's sweet-smelling bedroom. She flopped back on the bed and hiked up her skirt. I quickly shucked off my clothes.

"Wait a minute," she murmured, after I'd pulled off her

panties. She reached down and grabbed Patsy's photo and placed it on the nightstand, facing us. "I want Patsy to...to...be here with us. I want her to...*watch*..."

*T*wo days later we were out delivering and the receipt for the next order read, "Lavigne."

"Holy shit, Donzo, is that Lara Lavigne? Porter Ranch?"

"I think so. Let's see the address. Yep, Porter Ranch."

"You know who that is, don't you?"

"I'm afraid I don't."

"Lara Lavigne, the movie star. *Lair of the White Worm? Dance of the Damned?* She was real big in the late 80s, early 90's, back round the time of the..."

"The Northridge quake?"

"Yeah, right around there. She's a little past her prime now, but still a knockout. She's got a star at Grauman's Chinese, you know. The Walk of Fame. *Lara Lavigne*... I caddied for her once at the country club in Tarzana. She gave me a five hundred dollar tip. Don't count on her being home, though. She's probably out getting her ashes hauled."

We drove to the address and rang the bell. A maid answered the door. "Yes, please, gentlemen, bring it into the kitchen." Mickey and I hoisted the bags and marched into the palatial house, and suddenly, there in the kitchen, stood Lara Lavigne—*the* Lara Lavigne—in her tennis whites and her country club sweater, salon tanned, blonde and blowzy, a little drunk, maybe, and *bored*, bored out of her skull, and just itching for action.

"Listen, guys," she said, catching my arm, "do you know anything about washing machines? I've got one that's on the blink, and if you can do anything at all, I'd be very grateful."

She pinched my arm and gave me a melting look. I gave dear drunk Mickey a nudge: *keep the engine running, guy. I'll be there as soon as I can.*

Mickey got the message and retired to the van and I followed close behind Lara, Lara Lavigne, blonde, bouncy, tanned, rapacious. God, she smelled good! Even as she was leading me toward the laundry room I offered up a prayer of thanks. *Thank you, Heavenly Father. This is the realization of every delivery boy's most cherished masturbation fantasy.* At the same time, I was astonished. Lara Lavigne, *the* Lara Lavigne, doing her own laundry? Amazing!

We were standing close together now, confronting the stalled machine.

"Here's the problem. The drum doesn't seem to be rotating. Maybe there's something wrong with the timing. Listen, do you want a Vicodin? I've got a bottle of vodka in the freezer."

"Just a glass of water will be fine, Miss Lavigne."

"I can't figure out what's wrong with this damn thing. Maybe somebody just needs to tickle the wires a little bit."

"Tickle the wires?" *Holy Christ!* I took a chance and buried my nose in her hair. "I think I could tickle the wires, Miss Lavigne."

"Maybe you could just work it around—or poke it—or something."

"Sure."

"Do you know how to rotate the drums?"

"Oh, Jesus," I whispered, kissing her ear. I held her close and felt her tight ass.

"Baby," she whispered, "I'm wet for you. I want you to suck me off. Will you do it? What's your name?"

"Donald. My name is Donald..."

"Donald, will you kiss my pussy?"

"Yes, Miss Lavigne, I want to. I want to kiss you down there."

We yanked her tennis shorts down and her pink panties and she flopped back on a pile of dirty clothes and I knelt and stuck my tongue up her pussy and licked her up and down until she squirted off in my mouth.

"Oh, that was beautiful, darling." She hugged me and

kissed me again and again. "I love to taste myself on your lips," she murmured. "Now, do you want me to do something to you? I could kiss you down there, if that's what you like."

I didn't have to be asked twice.

Lara Lavigne, *the* Lara Lavigne, raised herself up on her elbow on the pile of dirty laundry, and I stood up and poked my dick into her mouth.

"*Umm...*"

I lasted about ten seconds. Mickey was tooting the horn, and she sure tooted *my* horn. It was exquisite, and all through it, as I watched her mouth moving on me, I was thinking, I'm having sex with Lara Lavigne, *the* Lara Lavigne, the bitchiest, most uppity girl in town, and it's wonderful—and not only that but at this very moment all across America thousands of underclass louts like myself are delivering groceries and flowers and pizzas to upscale neighborhoods, and each and every one of those lumpen sad-ass goons is dreaming the same sweaty proletariat dream, the archetypal delivery boy's wet dream, and here I am in Reseda and I'm living the dream—living it, actually living it—in the flesh.

After I squirted on her face she wiped my dick off on her tennis sweater and tucked it back into my shorts.

"Will you come back and see me again? What was your name? Daniel? Darren?"

"Donald."

"Okay, Daryl. I usually do my laundry on Tuesdays or Thursdays."

14

One day at the Goat Farm a strange thing happened. Norma—Norma Jacoby, my editor at Bareback Books— descended upon us. She took me completely by surprise and I felt like an idiot. I was drenched with sweat. I'd been chasing runaway goats all morning.

"So this is where you've been hiding out," she said haughtily. I thought she was going to give me a lecture but after she'd calmed down a she made me an offer I couldn't refuse: all rights to two of my best sellers, *Virgin Vixens of the Vatican* and *Nancy's Night with Noriega*—on the condition that I'd come back to work. These paperbacks of mine had climbed the porn charts back in the day but I'd gotten nothing because there was no royalties agreement. Having to crank out this schlock to make a living is bad enough but when you worked for Bareback Books as a final humiliation your contract read "Author for Hire." But now, Norma informed me, *Nancy's Night with Noriega* was going into its fourth printing and I'd own the rights, and if I had the good sense to get on board I'd clean up for sure. Moreover, I'd go back to getting advances, she said, and she'd put me on a royalties contract.

"It's the rebirth of Bareback Books, Donaldo. We're moving into the ebook market. Amazon Kindle, Nook, Google, it's breaking wide open. Listen to me. You were Orgasmo once and now you'll be Orgasmo again."

"In a pig's ass I will," I almost said, but Norma wouldn't have understood, and besides there was no way I was going to say no. "Holy shit," I muttered. "Porn on Amazon. It really is a new century."

"I don't call what we do porn, Donaldo," Norma said tartly. "We publish erotic novels. By the way, you won't have to write BDSM any more. Pompeii Press is merging with Lesbos Literary Classics..."

"What about Cliff English?"

"Cliff? Cliff's always been a pain in the ass, as you know. Cliff has delusions of grandeur. Cliff thinks we're Grove Press and he's Barney Rossett, but Cliff's a damn fine editor and we're moving him up to Acquisitions and he'll have his own office and a secretary, so I think he'll calm down."

Norma had the paperwork with her. We signed everything and she gave me my copies. I felt great but I felt awful too. I was letting myself down, and worse, I was letting my best pal Fausto down, after we'd solemnly pledged that day at the Wilshire Royale to quit writing and live normal lives. This was the Temptation in the Desert and I had succumbed. I didn't tell Norma about the Rimbaud Option. She wouldn't have understood. Norma was no longer a writer, if in fact she ever was one. Norma was a businesswoman. Her novel *Beyond the Burma Road* was gathering dust in a drawer somewhere and there it would stay. I knew that and I think Norma knew it too in her heart.

As we were shaking hands Norma said she was giving me a month to transition out of my job at the goat farm.

"I want you to write a sequel to *Nancy's Night*. Clean it up a little bit for Amazon, go light on the bestiality, but keep the jungle angle, and maybe put in some ritual cannibalism. You might also want to key in the Mayan 2012 Prophesy. Just a thought. And Che Guevarra's hot now after that big deal with *The Motorcycle Diaries.* Anyway, just start thinking along those lines, okay, and I'll see you in a month."

*D*oreen popped up. It had been how long? I couldn't be sure, but I took her reappearance as a harbinger, a sign that I would soon be living a normal life. I didn't ask about Harvey. We started going to the movies again, and we went for chili cheeseburgers at Tommy's and pastrami sandwiches at Canter's and out to see Gandhi's ashes at the Self Realization Shrine. We poked around Chinatown and we drank brown bag wine with Mad Rosa the Flower Lady on a bench in Lafayette Park. We seemed to get along okay. We were both being cautious, I guess.

We began hanging out with friends, going to parties. Doreen was great with people. She captivated them right away. She had the Tony Robbins patter down, Actualizations, Dr. Oz, Norman Vincent Peale... She'd been to a few nudist camps, had done the sweat lodge bit, the Taos thing and the past lives workshops; she'd been a Rolfing coach, a Reiki instructor, a pastry cook and a lifeguard, and she was into aromatherapy, numerology, shaman drumming, Feng Shui and Mahanaya Buddhism. All this ran pretty much automatically. Doreen was a transmitter, a conductor, a conduit. The words flowed out of her and events flowed through her. She knew she was special but she didn't know quite how to package herself.

I often wondered if Doreen had a heart but I noticed that she appeared to feel a twinge of anguish sometimes when she talked about her lost loves. The book was growing; I was churning out the pages—her autobiography, "The Oomph Girl." We'd go for sfogliatelle and rum babas at Mocafe, a friendly little place with outside tables corner of Santa Monica and Fairfax, and fuelled with cappuccino and mocha lattes, we'd jaw endlessly about the book. "The Oomph Girl" was turning out to be a much bigger job than I'd bargained for and I wanted to weasel out of it but I didn't know how. Doreen talked and talked and talked. The woman must have driven Harvey crazy.

Doreen's greatest asset was her enormous confidence. Doreen didn't let being thirty-eight stand in her way. She was a rising star, she was going places. Doreen saw herself that way and she had a way of making you believe it too. LA journalist Monica Seyfried once said of Doreen that, "She seems always to be shaking a tambourine." Doreen saw herself streaking across the sky, lighting up the world. The men she left behind her were fading sparks swirling in the wake of a great comet. She was the Oomph Girl, never out of character, always on stage. Others existed only as atoms to spin around her glowing nucleus. We were molecules to her, the rest of us, and me especially because I had somehow entered her orbit. She'd taken a shine to me, as one might to a spaniel. But why me out of all the nuggets in the pan? It was the writing, undoubtedly. She needed a scribe, an amanuensis. That had to be it. I was her Boswell. She was talking and I was writing it down in the Twelve Tablets. Finally we moved back in together, the place on Mariposa Street.

As the weeks passed and we settled into a routine, I began calling Doreen "Mama Kangaroo," because she carried me to all the outback waterholes in her fuzzy pouch, and fed me and bathed me and burped me, and all I had to do was copy everything down on my little slate.

A month or two went by and we were happy, but things took a turn for the worse, or so it seemed, when Crimini showed up, Gianni Crimini from Ruby Fine's lawn party in Westwood. I'd be typing and I'd hear the stealthy purr of the Porsche Spyder's engine. I'd pull back the curtains and peer out and there she'd be, Doreen, getting into the car, and never a word of goodbye or anything. I guess she thought I was too dumb or too wrapped up with my work on the book to notice—anyway, she'd come home later that night or sometimes the next morning coked out of her mind and freshly fucked. It didn't take a Sherlock Holmes to figure out what was going on.

When I confronted her, however, she was very up front about everything and I got the impression that she wasn't all that crazy about Gianni; she was just playing along hoping to get a part in one of his flicks. And Gianni wasn't Italian after all, she informed me; that is, he was Italian but he wasn't *Italian* Italian from Italy. He spoke Italian fluently and owned a restaurant in Newport, Gianni's Clam Bar. And he was more of a producer than a director, she said. And like Harvey, the used car salesman from Bellflower, Gianni had stomach problems.

"He's always *burping*," she'd complain, making a sour face. "*Blaap! Blaap!* Always popping those fucking Gas-X pills. It must be my pheromones. I always seem to attract men with Irritable Bowel Syndrome."

All the same, I was plenty nervous about trying to assert my mating rights for the simple reason that this Mafia hump might decide to have me whacked if he saw me as a rival for Doreen's affections. So I figured I'd see if I could make Doreen jealous instead. I called up the Goat Girls from Reseda and invited them to meet Doreen and myself for a drink at the Blue Monkey in Hollywood. Delia, the romance novelist, wasn't much of a party girl, but the other two, golden-eyed Dolly and Biruté from Belgium, were down for it. I told Doreen I wanted her to meet a couple of fellow actresses, perfectly true because Dolly had done that flushable tampon commercial and Biruté had played Desdemona in summer theater. And because I was practically broke I invited Fausto along, hoping he'd shell out for the drinks. I didn't tell Fausto about my plan to make Doreen jealous, but I figured to set him up with Biruté from Belgium and I'd put some moves on Flushable Tampon Dolly and see if Doreen would take the bait.

The next night Doreen and I arrived at the Blue Monkey by taxi. I was relieved to learn that there was no cover charge, and even more relieved when the bartender suggested that we run a tab. It would be much easier to break the news to Fausto that he had to spring for the drinks later on when he was sloshed.

After just one round of drinks Dolly and Biruté sailed in the door and we all sat down at a table. I made the introductions and the three aspiring actresses got into an excited tête-à-tête just as Fausto phoned to tell me that he was tied up with a Minnesota blonde and would be along soon. Then I butted into the girl talk and built Fausto up to Biruté, the six languages, the race car driver, the *fútbol* star, etc, conveniently leaving out the fact that Fausto was a hack writer, a pornographer and didn't have a pot to piss in.

We started out conservatively enough with what Doreen and I were drinking, Champagne Cocktails, but soon switched to Singapore Slings and Lime Rickeys, and finally, because Dolly insisted, Zombies.

Then—a surprise—Gianni Crimini walked into the Blue Monkey, followed by a sinister bodyguard, a real mouth breather with a boxer's flattened nose and a sour puckered look, as if he'd just swallowed a rectal suppository. Gianni and I had never been introduced and I didn't know what if anything Doreen had told him about me, but when we shook hands he was affable as a Methodist minister and he seemed to take to me right away. Still I was nervous and to be honest just plain scared. The phrase "*bocio di morte*" was going through my head as I recalled from the movies that your Cosa Nostra guys are always real nice to you just before they clip you in order to throw you off guard. But on the good side, I realized, I wouldn't have to ask Fausto to take care of the tab because Gianni was peeling crisp Benjamins off his gangster's roll right and left and ordering drinks for everybody at the bar.

Doreen proudly introduced Gianni the Movie Producer

to Flushable Tampon Commercial Dolly and Summer Theater Biruté, and I began to think that maybe I didn't need Fausto after all, maybe Biruté and Gianni would hook up, leaving me with Doreen and Dolly, and I'd charm the shit out of Dolly while Doreen turned six shades of green and the shoe, by Jesus, would be on the other foot for a change. And golden-eyed Dolly, Dolly the golden-eyed lioness, would be mine... There's something almost tender about the way a real, actual lioness kills a wildebeest on the Serengeti by closing off its windpipe with a gentle bite. I pictured the scene in my mind with myself as the wildebeest and Dolly as the lioness. Held down by Dolly's big floppy paws, I'd feel her warm breath on my face, hear her throaty growl; I'd look up into her impassive golden eyes, and then I'd feel her gentle jaws closing around my throat. How sweet it must be to die that way, I was thinking, to be devoured by a golden-eyed lioness on the Serengeti Plain. But when the girls went to the powder room and came back coked out of their gourds it became clear to me that Gianni was handing out the nose candy and would most likely walk away with all three of the dollies.

But Doreen was right about the stomach business, I have to tell you that. Just moments after Gianni sat down with us the pug with the flattened nose walked over and plunked a bottle of Pepto-Bismol down on the table and Gianni took a big swig and let out a loud belch. That was a shocker. I mean, I can't for the life of me picture Carlo Gambino knocking back huge slugs of Pepto-Bismol or Big Paul Castellano either for that matter. Those guys were made out of much sterner stuff. It's the times once again, this apocalyptic clusterfuck of a 21st century. Pesticides, pollution, the fake-ass vegetables they give you to eat—the human constitution simply isn't what it used to be.

"Donald writes dirty books," Biruté announced in a loud voice, jerking her thumb at me, addressing not only Gianni but everybody else in the bar. Then without further ado she proposed a pissing contest to see who could tell the best dirty story.

Of course Doreen had to lead off. "I've got a story to tell," she announced breathlessly. She downed her Zombie in a single gulp and cleared her throat, still breathless and obviously more than a little nervous, "I want you to hear me out. I promise you won't be disappointed."

"Go for it!" Biruté encouraged.

Doreen took a deep breath. "One time back when I was in high school in Pacoima this tramp came to the back door," she began. "My mom and my step dad were away. I was alone in the house. The tramp asked me if he could have something to eat. I invited him into the kitchen and made him a peanut butter and jelly sandwich. Then he asked me if he could take a bath. I said yes. I showed him the bathroom and got him some towels. A minute later—I was watching TV—he calls out to me. Could I come in and scrub his back? So I did. Boy, that bathwater was *black!* So I let the dirty water out of the tub and ran some clean water in. Then he asked me if I'd like to get in the bathtub with him. I says to myself, what's the harm of it? So I shucked off my shorts and halter and got into the tub with him. After a moment he said that he wanted to have his way with me. *Well, I wasn't going to pass up a chance like that!* We started to get into what you might call a compromising position in the bathtub, and suddenly his yogurt hose went off and..."

Doreen's voice trailed off.

"What's the matter?" Dolly put in.

"I don't know," Doreen said, shaking her head. "Maybe I can't do this after all..."

"Bullshit!" Dolly exclaimed. "You're doing fine. Don't think about what you're going to say. That's the secret of it. Right, Donald? You're a writer. Don't think. Just let the words come."

"Actually, there was just one more thing I wanted to add," Doreen interrupted.

"Sure, go ahead."

"It was a beautiful experience, and I know that someday when I'm old and gray I'll gather my grandchildren and great grandchildren around me and tell them about it and tears will come to my eyes."

"Beautiful," Gianni remarked. "Absolutely fucking beautiful."

"Thanks, Mr. G," Doreen murmured.

I was frosted. "So it's Mr. G now, is it?" I was thinking. "Christ Almighty! This is fucking bullshit..."

Then Fausto walked in, and the chemistry between Fausto and Dolly was instantaneous, as any idiot might have predicted, and I could see that my plan to make Doreen jealous by hitting on Dolly was going straight into the toilet. As Fausto hoisted his drink in that supremely confident manner of his, Dolly and Biruté were practically ripping the pants off him with their eyes, and although I tried my best to remain unruffled, I couldn't help thinking, "Christ, how unfair life is!" Here's this guy with cuties up the ass, Minnesota blondes by the metric ton, and he walks into the bar cold sober and immediately every girl in the Blue Monkey is practically dying to suck his dick. Full of pheromones, this bastard. It's genetics, the luck of the draw.

To make matters worse, Fausto, despite my careful spadework, wasn't all that taken with Biruté. "She smells like a goat," he hissed in my ear as he settled into his chair.

A moment later Vladimir happened by, Vladimir the café singer. Everybody knew Vladimir. He was a familiar figure in the bars all over town, ranging from Hollywood to the Rampart Precinct. Not young but classically handsome and deeply tanned, he was always very carefully turned out with his long silvery mane elaborately coiffed and sprayed, and a white Basque shepherd's shirt open at the throat exposing sculptured shaved pecs and a gold medallion. I knew Vladimir back in the Wilshire Royale days. He'd often sing at the bar, serenading the Japanese tourist ladies, and sometimes he'd get lucky and drag one of the geisha girls off to his dismal room at the Bryson. He'd do the old Jerry Vale numbers, the ultra-romantic stuff, "I Have But One Heart," "Arrivederche Roma," etc. Thoroughly European in dress and manner, Vladimir was Russian—or Polish—or Lithuanian—or Yugoslavian—he told you something different every time. The story of his life, or rather of the story of his lives, was included in his tableside serenades, and the story went on for as long as you'd continue to buy him drinks.

Meanwhile, Gianni had buttonholed me and was bending my ear, the man-to-man stuff, feeling my muscles, thumping me on the back, etc. "You're a big guy. Are you Russian by any chance? No offense."

"None taken, Mr. Crimini."

"Hey, call me Gianni, for chrissakes! Jesus, Donald! Is that your name, Donald? You know, you remind me of the wrestler, Krusher Kovalevski. You must have seen him on TV. I used him in one of my films. Big guy, crazy guy. You know what? I'm gonna call you D, Big D. Okay, D?" And on and on like that. I'd been prepared to thoroughly dislike this man who I considered to be an arrogant little prick, but he seemed to sincerely like me, and I have to say that the feeling was beginning to be mutual. This Gianni Crimini, this garrulous little mushroom of a man, wasn't such a bad egg after all. In fact, he was a damn nice guy, at least for a hardened criminal, and I actually thought that if I'd been halfway Sicilian or even halfway Italian he would have invited me to join the borgata.

Doreen had apparently told him something about me because he knew I was a writer. "Half of my fuckin' screenwriters are fuckin' faggots," he shouted above Vladimir's crooning voice. (Vladimir, smelling money, had waded in and was going full bore on "Arrivederche Roma.") Would you believe that? But not you, Big D. You're a frickin' stand up guy. A man's man. That's obvious. You served in the army. Don't ask me how I knew that. I got an intuition about these things. Probably played a little ball too. Right, Big D? Eh? Eh? Now I know who you remind me of—Hemingway! A writer should go marlin fishing. Don't you agree? He should hunt rhinos, he should go to the bullfights. You like the bullfights, Big D?"

"Fuckin' A, Gianni. It's all I ever do."

"That's my man!"

I should mention that there was perhaps something not quite real about Vladimir. As Vladimir finished up the last chorus of "Arrivederche Roma" and launched into "That Old Feeling," I found myself suddenly recalling the time, back in the Wilshire Royale days, when Vladimir, taken ill, handed me a ten-dollar bill at the bar and requested that I bring a bowl of Dante's homemade clam chowder to his room at the Bryson, formerly a haunt of the stars during Hollywood's Golden Era but now a seedy residence hotel.

When I arrived at Vladimir's room with the soup, some crackers and a six pack of PBR, he was lying on his rickety bed, deathly pale under his tan, with a sooty trickle of mascara running down his cheek from one dramatically arched eyebrow. A 40-watt bulb dangling from a frayed, knotted cord dimly illuminated a hotplate, stacks of dirty dishes, and on a hanger near a tiny window which afforded a view of a brick wall, the white Basque shepherd's shirt and the gold medallion. Without his iconic uniform Vladimir looked older, much older, and somehow naked, like a lobster that's been shucked out of its shell. He sat up in bed and drank the soup and it appeared to put some color in his cheeks, but he seemed to have lost his accent, and in fact he no longer looked European. Putting two and two together I realized that Vladimir had probably been born in LA, and that his real name was most likely something like "Jeremy Bosworth," and although it was rather sad to see him sitting in that sordid little room on the edge of his unmade bed in his white undershirt, with his spindly legs sticking out of striped boxer shorts and a Pabst Blue Ribbon beer in his hand, it was also a tribute to the power of the imagination, because if my suspicions were correct—and even at this juncture I'm not entirely sure that they were—Vladimir the café singer—suave, sophisticated, a sort of international roué—was a character that Jeremy Bosworth had created. A sparkling achievement too, if you ask me, because he'd literally pulled himself up by his own bootstraps. He had *imagined* himself.

"Hey guys, I've got a story for you," Gianni said. Jovially drunk, he was perched between Fausto and me with an arm draped around each of us. The girls went to the can for another bump of Colombian marching powder and Doreen, in passing, whispered, "*Psst! Don't let him talk your ear off. He's obsessed with his bowel movements!*"

But it was too late; Gianni was already off and running. "When I was twelve years old my pops took me on this trip to Europe, and oh my God I got so frickin' constipated! I couldn't walk two steps without keeling over from the pain. I'm telling you, it was the worst fuckin' thing I ever experienced. So here we are in this fuckin' gondola going through the Swiss Alps, and Pops gives me this laxative, see, and the whole frickin' mass down there in the large intestine finally begins to move. I pulled up my shirt and you could see it, like a fuckin' giant worm crawling under the skin, peristalsis in action, baby, a living, writhing snake. *Whoom!* And *whoom-ba-doom!* I could feel it building up, rumbling around in my guts like Vesuvius and Krakatoa and Mount Kilamanjaro all rolled into one."

Gianni paused for a hit of Pepto-Bismol and the girls returned from the john as Vladimir started in on "Pretend You Don't See Her." Both Dolly and Doreen, drunk as skunks and coked to the max, joined in and began singing along with Vladimir. The two of them were blinking back tears, and even the bartender's eyes were moist, I noticed.

"And would you believe it, the fuckin' restroom was locked."

"Hmm, that was unfortunate. To say the least..."

By now somebody had killed the jukebox and everybody in the bar was listening raptly as Vladimir sang "I Have But One Heart." By the second chorus a lot of them had joined in and were singing along, and soon there wasn't a dry eye in the place. I swear I'm not exaggerating. A dewy sentimental mood had engulfed the Blue Monkey, and I was astonished at how readily the bar crowd abandoned their revelry and jolly talk and latched onto it. It was as if they'd been waiting all their lives for a chance to have a good cry.

Gianni resumed, shouting above the singing. "So I goes back to Pops and he's sitting there with his whiskey and soda four sheets to the wind, and he doesn't give a fiddler's fuck, you know. Just stick your ass out the window and let 'er go, he says. What the fuck, I says. Dad, I can't do that, I says. Stick my ass out the window and shit all over the Swiss Alps? Dad, I can't frickin' do that! But, by the grace of God, the boghouse door opened up right about then. I made a beeline for it and plopped down on the throne and this French cunt comes in and sits down right beside me. That's the way they do things in France, you know. She mumbles something in French and reaches across me sorta-like. Jesus, D, I thought she was making a grab for the old wazoo! You know? Well today, hell, today I would have told her, hey, put your hand on *this*, sister! Voulez vous suckie my dickie, por favor? But, Holy Christmas, guys, I was only twelve years old and besides, by now the goddamn lava was starting to flow. The critical mass—the critical mass, amigos—was on the move down there in the intestinal environment. The old transverse colon was undergoing peristaltic contractions and that motherfucker was getting ready to go *kaboom! Kaboom!* And *Whoom-ba-doom-ba-doom!* The seismic convulsions were beginning, and believe me, it was right off the Richter Scale!"

Fausto shot me a pleading look: *let's get the fuck out of here, man!* But there was no way we could do that, not with Mr. G sitting between us and running off at the mouth the way he was. Fausto was spooked, and so was I if I'm going to be honest, but at the same time I was positively delighted at how chummy Gianni and I were becoming, and I was even considering trying to touch him for a small loan right then and there, but of course on the other hand I didn't want to crowd my luck.

"Fantastic, Gianni," I murmured.

"Yeah, well, Big D, as it turned out, this French cunt just wanted to borrow some toilet paper. So, I'm sitting there on the throne and I'm thinking in my twelve-year-old mind, is this right? I mean etiquette-wise? Is it right to take a dump in front of a lady? Because she was a lady, Big D. This was one of your fuckin' Veronica Verekova types with Tiffany diamonds up the ass and a Max Factor beehive hairdo and Je t'adore sparkle dust all over her titties. Real fuckin' elegant, you know? But I said, the hell with it! Nature calls, guys! Open the floodgates! Tallyho! Let the games begin! Gentlemen, start your engines!"

A cell phone jangled and Crimini's bodyguard, who'd been standing at the bar, approached our table. Gianni stood up and the two conversed briefly, *sotto voce*, in Italian, then Gianni turned to us. "Fall by the restaurant, Big D!" he shouted, punctuating his words with a strident belch. "You too, Fausto!" You could tell he was disappointed— he obviously had a few *whoom-ba-doom-ba-dooms* left in him—but he blew kisses to the girls and stuffed a few bills down the front of Vladimir's shirt; then as he and his shadow made for the door, the palooka turned and shot me a murderous look—a bit over the top, I thought.

"These fucking Cosa Nostra pricks," Fausto remarked. "They've had so many fucking movies made about them they couldn't fucking break character if they wanted to."

Biruté left with Vladimir, and ten minutes later Dolly left with Fausto. *Of course!* They'd go back to his place or her place, and Dolly, the golden-eyed lioness, would become just another notch on Fausto's gun belt, "the one I pulled out of the Blue Monkey that night."

Doreen and I woke up the next morning in Vladimir's bathtub. We got a bit of a shock when Vladimir walked into the bathroom with his hands all bloody—so we thought—but it turned out it was beet juice. "Borscht," he announced. "I'm making borscht. Best thing in the world after a night of drinking. Better even than menudo."

Then Doreen and I got into an argument. Not about Mr. G—although there was plenty I wanted to say on that subject—but the thing was Doreen didn't want me to include the bit about spending the night in Vladimir's bathtub in the book, her memoir, "The Oomph Girl," because, she claimed, it made her look like a blackout drunk. I disagreed. "Nonsense," I said. "It's colorful. It's good theater."

"Yeah, but this is a sleazy part of town, Baby," she declared solemnly as she sprayed an armpit with a shot of Vladimir's Dolce & Gabbana. "Couldn't you move Vladimir's apartment to Beverly Hills?"
"Well...I suppose I could..."

15

Skylar invited me to a farewell Sunday brunch at the Beverly Hilton. He's off for his European spoken word tour. He'll be hitting the coffeehouses in London, Paris, Milan and Amsterdam. We sat near the caviar and prawns, almost exactly where I'd sat months earlier with Hugo van der Weyden, maybe even the same table. I was fast becoming a regular at 9876 Wilshire Boulevard, which the *Los Angeles Times* called, "One of the great places in the world to see and be seen." Our talk was brief; Skye had a plane to catch. After coffee and tiramisu he had his driver drop me off before he continued on to LAX.

"I keep coming back to Joyce's statement that *history is a nightmare from which I am trying to awake*," Skye said as we shook hands. "Maybe it wouldn't be such a fucking nightmare if women ruled the world. In distant ages when the Goddess reigned supreme, life was a sacred whole and humanity, the Earth and all life on Earth were woven into a single cosmic web. The world needs compassion, gentleness, nurturing—all feminine qualities. Cross-dressing and feminization are much more than just a quirk with me, Donald. Considering what the male hegemony has done to the earth and its peoples over the past five millennia, the wars and massacres and the destruction of the environment, one almost feels an obligation to become a woman."

16

*S*pring! The earth tilts on its axis, flowers bloom, groundhogs come out, birds migrate, fish return to spawning grounds and people fall in love. April has arrived and Fausto's flying high. He got a speaking part in indie horror director Oskie Oldham's new slice-and-dice, *Spurned, Slashed and Burned.* At first Fausto was sure he was going to play the Latin lover, but now it turns out that he's playing the bad guy, in a rubber swamp monster suit.

"It's still a speaking part," Fausto insisted as we downed a few Modelos at La Pachanga. Come to find out they're going to have Fausto improvise some growls and roars, stuff like, "GRRROW! OOOOG! AAARGH!" His voice will be muffled, he admits, inside that vulcanized rubber monster suit, especially if he's under five or six feet of swamp water, but his enthusiasm is utterly undampened and he's certain in his heart of hearts that he's Antonio Banderas. His eyes flash dangerously as he plays the bongo drums, and he'll go up to a strange woman in a bar and inquire fiercely, "What are your *passions?*" Fausto's always had the looks, no question about that, but now he's got the panache.

When Doreen got wind of Fausto's audition of course she was going to read for the part of the heroine, she who was Spurned, Slashed and Burned. "Baby I am ready to rip and roar," she shouted as she sailed out the door of the place on Mariposa Street. But she got to the set too late and the director had already hired a much younger actress. But then the guy gave Doreen the job of making some fake movie blood, and the next day at Mariposa Street I helped her brew five gallons of the stuff using corn syrup, peanut butter and Black Cherry Kool-Aid. After a romp in the hay and lunch at Tommy's Doreen borrowed a girlfriend's car and we drove out to the set, an abandoned barn in West Fallbrook. I met the director, Oskie Oldham, an intense little man whose close-set black eyes festered like inquisitive raisins. He ordered another five gallons of fake blood and told me he'd be interested in seeing a script if I could come up with something involving a band saw.

On our next trip to West Fallbrook with the blood, we stopped into a local burger joint and the waitress told me about a job. A demolition crew, she said, was tearing down the old Fallbrook Hotel, and the site was just a stone's throw away, and they needed workers. That was good news, because Doreen and I were pretty hard up, a month behind on the rent and what have you. Then Oldham fixed things so that Doreen and I could stay in one of the trailers on the set of *Spurned, Slashed and Burned*, and that clinched the deal. I think he mostly did it to keep Doreen around. Oskie Oldham didn't understand that you don't keep Doreen around. Doreen keeps you around.

Doreen and I spent several lazy days in the trailer while we waited to see if I was going to get hired. We were alone, except for the raccoons and possums that scampered over the roof at night. We spent a lot of time just firkytoodling around, not doing much of anything. After dinner we'd sit in our folding chairs with our Blue Ribbon beers and watch the night come down. "Just like regular people," Doreen would exclaim delightedly. The air was soft and filled with the honest smell of farm animals. Coyotes, too, you'd hear them setting up a howling chorus, some of them near, others far away, across a broad valley. They were talking to each other.

One night a full moon made me think of Starz. If he was still alive, he was probably wandering the streets of LA under that same full moon, or squatting in an alley drinking brown bag wine and trying to figure out where he'd gone wrong. Or maybe walking with his ratty suitcase through some bumfucked railroad yard, thinking about his kids calling him from Disneyland and wondering if he should put his head down on the tracks.

Starz was used up. Anybody could have seen that. He'd been drinking hard back at the big old house on Highland, and of course earlier on in Malibu. The talk we had at the pool the day before he vanished was excruciating. He'd been hot-knifing hash oil and his thoughts were coming a mile a minute. His kids weren't returning his calls. His family had disowned him. He had nerve damage in his hands from running the dish machine at the scullery. His money was gone. And he'd sold his camera. He kept repeating that part, "I fucking sold my camera, man! I can't believe I fucking sold my camera!" Then Tiffany rode off on a Harley with a Gypsy Bandit. But that wasn't it, losing Tiffany. Starz didn't care anything about Tiffany. And it wasn't the hands or the money. Starz had lost his identity, he'd lost his reason for being. "I've got a movie in me, homes." That's what he kept saying to me, "I've got a movie in me. I know I do." But the subtext to that, the question I knew he was asking himself was, "Am I a filmmaker who washes dishes to make ends meet or am I a dishwasher who used to be a filmmaker?" Starz was as desperate as any man who ever walked the earth. Selling his camera had killed him. It had broken him. Hollywood was far away now, more distant than the moon, even though in reality it was right across town. In a voice thick with tears he told me how he'd tried to commit suicide back in Ohio by driving his car into a bridge. He failed because he was drunk and ran into a soft embankment rather than the steel-reinforced concrete. He bailed out of a mental hospital in Cleveland, sold his computer, bought some crank and drove non-stop to LA, fueled with crystal meth. It was the Carrie Fisher book, *Shockaholic*, that made him decide to check into the Vet's Hospital and get the juice. Later as we were drinking Gallo zinfandel in the kitchen and I was making spaghetti, he told me, "I didn't have the money to put my furniture in storage when I got evicted so I chopped my bed up with an axe so it would fit in the dumpster." Starz was chopping everything up, his career, his marriage, his life, and now the doctors had chopped up his mind, fried whole sections of his brain, changed the neurons around, mixed everything up. He was terrified that they'd killed the artist in him. I never thought that would be possible. I never would have believed it. I'd always thought that Starz was indestructible. Starz, old Starz, you couldn't keep him down, he always bounced back, but maybe this time he wasn't going to bounce back, maybe not.

Two days later I got a call from the demolition company and the next morning I kissed Doreen goodbye at the front door of our trailer and she handed me my lunch in a brown paper bag. I felt just great. We were fast becoming regular people.

At the old Fallbrook Hotel site I was assigned to work with a man named Jesse. We worked underneath the building. Jesse was small and birdlike. He wore army khakis, rubber boots, and a World War I doughboy's hat with the brim pulled down over his eyes. We didn't do anything at all, I mean for days. Nothing was happening topside, either. A temporary work-stoppage order had come down from God knows where. From God, if you like. It was all the same from our point of view.

Underneath the floorboards Jesse and I crouch opposite each other in the black dirt. Jesse pulls a pint of

Old Heaven Hill out of his hip pocket. He tips the bottle up and guzzles like a bird. In the half darkness Jesse is almost invisible. He's a ghost, a wraith, an apparition. Only his eyes, dancing under the crumpled hat brim, are alive. His tiny bright eyes. They glisten like moist grubs as he swallows noisily and hands me the bottle.

Drinking from the bottle, I savor the moment. Dark all around me and the whiskey going down, the floorboards creaking above my head, and at our feet the picks and shovels and wrecking bars we've dragged into our underground lair. It's a beautiful moment.

Jesse's life, I learn, consists of such moments snatched from the sequence of the daily grind. He has twelve children, seven of them boys, five of them grown, none of them any good. One lad is doing time for rape, another is a murderer, the other three are thieves. Jesse lives in a shanty in West Fallbrook on the edge of a celery bog, raises pigs and chickens, never has the rent on time and drinks his paycheck on Friday night. All this Jesse tells me in a pleasant monotone as we squat in the black dirt passing the pint back and forth. Jesse has so many problems that he has no problems. Faced with mountainous obstacles he did a long time ago exactly what I would have done. He gave up. Jesse is so far down he has come through on the other side, on the other side of the human problem. For Jesse now there remain only the animal problems. Squatting comfortably on his haunches he tips the bottle up and swallows a mouthful of warm whiskey. He savors what there is to savor.

On the third day, around mid-morning, I eat a cucumber sandwich with mayonnaise, courtesy of Doreen. Jesse and I pass the bottle. Centipedes meander at our feet. Jesse scrapes the soft earth with the heel of his boot and uncovers a thick white grub with shiny black pincers.

"We used to eat those things when we were building the railroad in Panama," he whispers confidentially.

The floorboards creak above our heads. Time to look

busy. Jesse asks me in a pleasant whisper, that whiskey monotone of his, if I prefer to use the wrecking bar or the crowbar. It's mid-morning, you understand, and we haven't lifted a finger. I tell him I prefer the heavier wrecking bar because I feel sorry for the little bugger. And because I like his voice. It's a gentle voice, a whiskey voice with a bit of a burr to it.

Couching, I nudge with the wrecking bar at a rotten piling. The moist wood crumbles like sponge cake. Amazing. After a few moments Jesse holds up his hand. He cautions me not to do too much. We both listen intently. The floorboards overhead have stopped creaking. Most likely it was just some joker getting up to take a piss.

Our job... It's difficult to explain, since I don't profess to understand it. Bunch of red tape. We're to look busy, in case the boss comes around. This much, of course, I understand. *But how can we look busy if we're entombed under the floorboards?* At the same time, we can't dismantle anything, even to amuse ourselves. We're forbidden to even so much as pry a nail out of a board. Your red tape again. How to explain it? I'm not even interested. Far be it from me to question the order of things.

Jesse is rattling on in his raspy whiskey voice. I sit in the mud with my back resting comfortably against a rotten beam, the bottle in my mitt, letting Jesse's words wash over me while I watch a spider spinning her web on a joist above my head. *It's beautiful,* I'm thinking. I really am happy here. No matter what I fall into these days, I seem to come up smelling sweet.

Later. I swallow the last drink of whiskey and toss the empty bottle over my shoulder. Jesse grins under his crazy hat brim. He digs out another pint of Old Heaven Hill he has stashed in his boot. We drink whiskey. Three or four days go by like this. We don't do anything. Nothing happens. Occasionally the floorboards creak above our heads.

By the morning of the fourth day I'm beginning to feel

that maybe it's not so beautiful after all. We're insects, centipedes, white grubs. After three days under the floorboards with Jesse I feel like I'm in solitary. It's not that he doesn't *talk*, no, he does plenty of that, but he speaks a different language. He speaks a white-grub language.

And where are the other bozos, I find myself wondering, our co-workers upstairs who are supposedly gnawing away like boll weevils at the beams and rafters? Hiding away in the woodwork, no doubt, half dozing but ready like us to spring into action the instant the Grand Dragon comes rolling around. But when does the bastard come around? *Nobody* comes around, as far as I can see. Once in a while we hear the floorboards groaning above our heads and that's about it.

Jesse goes a long way back, I decide. He's older than I thought. No guessing his age, however. His teeth are brown. I sit staring at the wisps of smoke hissing between Jesse's teeth and I see a white grub, a centipede whose mandibles secrete brown tobacco juice. I shake my head, I blink my eyes, I try to calm myself. I'm getting stir crazy. But we can't go out until five o'clock. Those are the rules. The Imperial Wizard might be sliding by in his solid gold Cadillac. And one can't stand up to pee. The floor is too low above our heads. You squat to make water, like a brain-dead cockroach cowering under a sink drain. We're cockroaches, dung beetles, centipedes, salamanders, grubs. We're the lice that fester and itch under the Grand Dragon's dirty hide. We're doodles on an air-conditioned expense account. We're a jot and a squiggle on the shirt cuff of a white maggot who sits at a desk dialing telephone numbers.

Lousy bastards!

The hours pass slowly. We take turns sleeping. *Can I last until payday?* I watch the spiders spinning their intricate webs. *Such patience!* We line the empty whiskey bottles up in rows next to the pilings. *Dead soldiers.*

Every so often the whole hulking works jars off the foundations. Glass shatters and plaster dust filters down on our heads. It's not the guys working upstairs, no; it's the big guns booming at the artillery range a few miles west of here.

It was on a Wednesday, I recall, that the shelling began...

On Thursday a trip to the dump enlivens our routine. I drive the company truck. Jesse is too drunk to sit behind the wheel. On a backcountry road I swerve to avoid a Black Angus bull. The tarp blows off the back. Junk strews all over the road—boards, broken glass, hunks of plaster and drywall.

After I get the tarp tied back on and the trash picked up, a mile or so down the road, we have a flat. Girls in white blouses wave from passing cars as I wrestle the huge truck tire. Jesse is stretched out in the seat, snoring. It's a fine sunny day. The flower fields on both sides of the asphalt are blooming red, white and yellow. As we get moving again sweet aromas of fodder and manure tickle my nose. In the distance the guns are booming, louder now, since we're driving west. On the horizon a pillar of greasy black smoke rises, as if from a torpedoed ship: the dump.

We eat lunch at the dump, sprawled on the paint-spattered tarp in the warm sunshine. I've backed the rig up to the edge of the slope. My lunch, packed by Doreen, the Oomph Girl, consists of two liverwurst sandwiches and a pear. For two days now it's been liverwurst and mayonnaise sandwiches on porous white bread like cheesecloth. But it's bread, and bread is good. And I definitely prefer the liverwurst to the cucumbers. It's good to feel a piece of meat between your teeth now and then, even if it's only snips and snouts, hog rinds, pig's trotters and chicken assholes stewed up together and pressed into a loaf. *It's meat! It's good!*

Munching my sandwich, shooing aside the buzzing

hordes of green bottle flies, I watch the clouds of thick greasy smoke billow up from the chasm as smoldering bundles of newspapers shift like pedals in the fire. The dump master emerges from his shack, stoop-shouldered, grimy as a coal miner, carrying a wide-toothed wooden rake. He does a standing glissade over the edge of the chasm. Halfway down he whirls, plants himself thigh-deep in steaming garbage and begins to rake the perpetually falling slope of smoldering dreck and ruin. The fire banks down; a section of the slope shears away in an avalanche of clattering tin cans and soot-blackened bottles clanking together. Charred scraps of newspaper fly up from the red-orange cholera-boil of eggshells, fizzing grapefruit, murdered dolls, sputtering rags and curling banana rinds. Bottles explode, rats burst like grenades, light bulbs pop, and occasionally you hear a muffled *chug* as a jar of rancid mayonnaise buried deep in the mix goes off like a depth bomb.

Jesse is tapping me on the shoulder. My turn to drink from the bottle. The plan is to remain at the dump until quitting time. Here, Jesse assures me, we'll be safe from Mr. Big. The rat bastard is too cheap to pay the three-dollar admission fee.

Gazing through the smoky haze into the abyss, I bite into my last liverwurst sandwich. The fire flares fiercely, like a raw wound. The stink makes my eyes water. The sun is blistering hot. I unbutton my shirt. My sandwich is sopping with mayonnaise. It's like biting into a fresh compress. I try my best not to think about it. The wind shifts and I get a facefull of coarse gritty soot. My gorge is rising. I'm beginning to think that maybe we were better off under the floorboards.

Jesse is going on in his thin whispery voice, something about payday being a couple days off. Looking at Jesse, I can't help wondering if the poor blighted bastard will make it to payday. His voice is getting fainter, for one thing. The sunlight seems to be disintegrating him. Suddenly a series of trip-hammer explosions rocks the truck off its chocks. The big guns are booming again on the horizon. The Poet Laureate of Death is testing out his *terza rima*.

I finish my sandwich and bite into the pear. The pear is rotten. I throw the pear into the abyss. The dump master looks up at me, his face and forearms glistening with wet garbage. He shouts something incoherent. He waves. I wave back. He laughs uproariously, slapping his thigh. I laugh too. He grins and sputters, rolling his eyeballs skyward. Evidently the man is an imbecile.

Jesse shoves the bottle at me. I take a last long swallow of Old Heaven Hill. It glows raw and warm all the way down. I toss the empty bottle over my shoulder into the chasm. *Another dead soldier!*

Saturday rolls around, that's payday. "Good day for sleeping," Jesse remarks wearily, letting out a huge shuddering sigh. I nod my head. My mouth is dry. We drink wine all day.

Afternoon. The sun's rays are slanting under the beams into our spider's lair. I take off my shirt and ball it up for a pillow. I take a snooze. I wake up. Jesse is squatting in front of me on the baked clay, holding his watch in the palm of his hand. He gives me a jerk of his chin, his eyes dancing like faint sparks under the scoutmaster's scarecrow hat brim.

"*Five o'clock!*" he whispers merrily.

On my hands and knees, hooking the half-empty jug of red wine along with one finger, I crawl out from under the building. As I stand erect for the first time in eight hours, stretching my arms to the sky, the world rushes up to greet me, the cars, the people, a blinking orange beer sign, a girl on horseback clattering up a hill. The pink sky is glowing softly, like an uncut gem. Jesse looks up at me and grins. *What's a few more minutes now?* We're in no hurry, either of us, to do anything, not even to collect our pay. *Fuck it!* When the butterfly emerges at last from its cocoon, aren't the very air and the sunlight itself enough to dazzle him?

We finish off the wine, get our money at the guard shack and take a taxi to Club 99. Then we hit the Shamrock Club, and then the Coral Seas, where Jesse pours quarters like a fiend into the slot, singing and hiccupping and dancing all alone in the orange-green jukebox glow while the broken-toothed barmaid in her skinny red dress and white cowboy hat sways to the twang of syrupy guitars, clapping her hands and urging him on. From the Coral Seas we head back to Club 99, where we get the heave-ho, then it's the Shamrock Club again, and finally we wind up at the Tradewinds, drunk as skunks, and Jesse's old lady, a frightful harridan in a bile-green dress, comes and drags us out.

Now I'm sitting at a table in the kitchen of Jesse's reeking clapboard shanty. *We eat:* white rice boiled in suet, scrambled powdered eggs with a greenish tinge, instant mashed potatoes, day-old bread and welfare peanut butter. Commodity foods, everything tasteless, soupy, like wallpaper paste. The hulking wife, cursing like a drill sergeant, cigarette glued to her lips, doles it up with a huge soup ladle. She curses Jesse, she curses the kids, she curses me. She drags the sleeve of her dress in the kettle and she curses that.

This is the jungle, I tell myself. This is the heart of darkness, a festering sinkhole where black orchids bloom in the dead of night. The domain of the tsetse fly, a heaven of putrefaction and mold. The sloth calling to its mate in three feet of swamp water.

The disarray is incredible. Ducks and squawking roosters strut through the two grimy rooms as if they owned the place. The kids eat sitting on the bare-boards floor, balancing their plates of steaming slop on their laps. Throughout the meal they jabber and shriek like a troupe of monkeys. The little ones have the look of faded rags. Potato faces, pale chalky eyes, as if they've been soaked in lye and all the vitamins leached out of them, or boiled with dishrags and hung out to bleach in the sun.

Jesse and I eat in chagrined silence, like condemned men. Halfway through the meal the old lady takes Jesse's wad of bills out of her purse, what's left of his paycheck, and stuffs it down her sweaty bosom, this with a venomous look at me. *Don't worry, sister,* I feel like saying. *It's plenty safe there, as far as I'm concerned.*

I shovel the food in while a ragged hound, slouching under the table, nibbles at my toes. Moments later a gaunt ferocious hog trots briskly through the two rooms, in one door and out the other, snorting fiercely and nearly trampling a child and nobody so much as glances up.

Schlup, schlup, schlup!

Dessert is a plate of suet laced with sorghum or Karo syrup. It looks like afterbirth. I choke it down because I feel it's my duty to be polite. Jesse does the same. The dogs and pigs watch every bite that goes into our mouths.

After supper everyone sits around belching contentedly and picking their teeth with splinters pried up from the floor. Everyone except the old lady, that is. Already she's on her feet, filling the sink with Clorox. The TV screen flickers faintly, as if it contained a swarm of fireflies. In a corner a retarded lad wearing an orange propeller beanie is pulling himself off. A grimy baby, shaking her rattle, burps and coos. Suddenly pinfeathers are flying. One little devil has caught a rooster and has twisted its neck. The others close in for the kill...

I doze off... I wake up. I glance around the room. The old lady is peeling potatoes—for tomorrow. The hogs sit in a circle at her feet, waiting to snap up the parings. I close my eyes. Suddenly the floor under my feet gives a shudder. The swamp's rhythmic contractions are rattling the dry bones of the shack. Or maybe the big guns are booming again. The tin roof creaks, the crazy pictures on the wall jerk sideways, pots and pans clatter in the cupboards, the TV screen flickers out of kilter. I sense that we're slowly sinking into the muck.

Ruminating, shifting my cud, I peer at Jesse snoring

with his head on the supper table and the cockroaches scurrying over the plates. He's such a pipsqueak compared to her, I can't get over that. *The size of the woman!* The heft and girth of her, not to mention her towering height. It gives me the willies. *Poor Jesse.* It's as if she's squeezed all the sperm out of him and now he's collapsed on the table like a punctured bladder. But the kids he managed to fuck into existence, the idiots and murderers he sired. I can't help being impressed. It's a sort of negative triumph.

Half dozing in my chair, I study the family portraits on the wall, faces of imbeciles, faces of psychopaths, faces of Pithecanthropus men. As I drift in and out of sleep they pass in review, pederasts and pocket-pool fiends, bile-green monsters that should have died in the egg, dumb brutes sagging under the executioner's hammer. *Step right up!* The white trash Genesis, pellagra begat rickets begat *beriberi.* The scraps of meat that writhe on the slaughterhouse floor, the lips choked with spit, the heart choked with ice, the white hands that clutch at the plumes of departing flesh, the hopes that glitter like fragments of chewed glass on the tongue of a carnival god.

When the sky begins at last to give off a copper-kettle glow I get to my feet and tiptoe out of the shanty, leaving the sleepers to toot and wheeze like a family of bassoonists tuning up.

I walk west, the red sky behind me, until I hit the railroad tracks. Here, at the first sign of civilization, I instinctively check my poke. Squatting on the gravel bank overlooking the tracks, I unwad the crumpled bills and smooth them out. I count them. I still have 78 bucks and some change, I discover, after taxes and drinking. Doreen will be pleased, I'm thinking. Now I can buy her that vibrator she's been talking about.

Stepping along, I whistle a few bars of a tune, "I'll Take You Home Again, Kathleen," and last night comes rushing back. Jesse is pouring money into the jukebox. At the Shamrock Club, it was. We must have sung that song a dozen times. The whole bar was singing, everyone looped and the beer foaming over the rails, along with the schmaltzy music. What the heck. It's fun to have a good cry once in a while. Healthy, too. It cleans you out, like a diet of lentils or a dose of rancid suet pudding.

Birds are beginning to trill. I step briskly along. Amazing how still it is out here, wherever that is, I'm thinking, when the big guns aren't booming on the horizon. And when I reach the blacktop I know I'm right. The sun is peeping over the rim of a hill. A new day is dawning. I pause and shine my teeth on my soiled t-shirt. Walking along, I pat the golden egg in my pocket. I feel like I've just served a hitch in the Coast Artillery. *Bueno.* Yes! I stick out my thumb. *There'll be a ride along in a minute,* I tell myself. And whichever way I'm going I'll get there faster.

17

Back in LA Doreen and I watched the director's cut of *Spurned, Slashed and Burned* with Oskie Oldham, Fausto and lead actress Tatania Ferrari. "*Made with our gooey blood,*" Doreen whispered proudly, as a man with a meat cleaver chopped off a woman's left hand. "*This film was made with our gooey blood.*"

Fausto's swamp monster was both menacing and pathetic, a poignant combination, but his bestial grunts were not all they might have been, as Doreen and I privately agreed. He sounded too much like a man shouting at the top of his lungs inside a rubber monster suit. Nevertheless Oskie Oldham was pleased with the film and with Fausto's performance. Everyone agreed that Fausto died well, and Doreen was in fact weepy during the swamp monster's death scene in which strange ragged girls poked the creature's eyes out with ski poles. "That's our blood," she murmured through her tears as she squeezed my hand. "That's our fucking gooey blood."

I went for a meeting with Norma at the new office in

Hollywood Hills. The office was posh, not at all like the old days when Bareback Books was a stuffy hole in the wall above a tattoo parlor on Hollywood Boulevard and I'd have my story conferences with Norma at Gorky's over borscht and Russian beer. After our confab, which went swimmingly, Norma took me on a tour of the facility. Ruby Fine's office looked like the boudoir of some depraved sultaness. I can't begin to describe it. The vases, the tapestries, the bric-a-brac. An antique porcelain bidet, and an alabaster statue of the god Priapus with a tremendous erection, a stuffed cheetah and a live ocelot pacing in a cage, and to top it off, a honey-glazed terra cotta pisspot supposedly used by the mad emperor Elagabalus.

In the hallway, after bidding Norma goodbye, I ran into Cliff English. Unlike Norma Jacoby, Cliff hadn't given up the ghost. He still had the fire, and maybe even the talent. But a darkness had come over him lately, something grim, something sour, a fatalistic kismet-like mentality. He used the word "kismet" in fact at least three times during our conversation in the hallway. It was as if he'd recently discovered that it was irrevocably written in the heavens that he was doomed to spend the rest of his life crouching under the wallpaper. And his appearance...that too had changed, I noticed. With his carefully trimmed mustache and scotch-on-the-rocks complexion, he was a dead ringer for Papa Hemingway. Or maybe for one of Hemingway's famous noir heroes, spitting out terse-lipped gems of cynical sappy wisdom along with broken teeth, the quintessential iron-assed loser who despite repeated trips to the canvas still has that one last desperate shot at redemption.

Cliff English wasn't always soured on life. Testy, yes, cantankerous, sure, but he wasn't sour. In the old days, the Bareback Book days, when Cliff and Fausto and I were paid hacks in Ruby Fine's stable of purebred pornographers, we'd go out drinking together, and often we'd stop in for a few beers and the heavenly French dip sandwiches at Phillipe's near Union Station on the edge of Chinatown. We were all of us writers, all poor, and we were all crazy about Blake, Emily Dickinson and Joseph Conrad, the Polish sea captain who wrote *Heart of Darkness*. Our conversations at Phillipe's were electric back then, world-embracing. We had food and drink. Life was good. We were happy. But now...

"Do you want to go for a beer?" Cliff said laconically. We stepped outside and he flagged down a taxi. "No worries, I'll pay," he murmured. He seemed to have money and I could tell he wanted to talk. "Let's go to Maria's," he said. "It'll be just like old times."

At Maria's in Grand Central Market we start drinking Carta Blancas. Cliff is soon looped and bursting with talk about his stillborn novels. He has to get it out, the pain and bitterness and remorse he nurtures like a saint guarding a precious wound.

"Get this: I saw on Yahoo where several recent books have been channeled by some guy who lived in Egypt five thousand years ago. You know, maybe that's where I went wrong. I should have had an Egyptian mummy dictate my goddamn books. Instead, here I am writing *The Autobiography of Joe Shit the Ragman!* But that's the world for you, homes. You have to be dead for five thousand years before they'll listen to you. Grave robbers, that's what these people are. Why can't they write their own fucking books? *Kismet.* It's Kismet. Ever think about it? Ever think about your past lives? You could be born a prince or you could be born a pig or a duck or an ant. I know we have to play the hand we're dealt. But we don't have to like it. What about you, Donaldo? Who were you in your past life?"

"I don't know. Joe Shit the Ragman, I guess."

Cliff has a problem, vis a vis the writing, in that it takes him all day to write a paragraph. He agonizes over phrases. It's not that the well had dried up. It's a simple case of constipation. He needs a laxative, a verbal high enema. Back in the old days, Cliff, *viva voce*, at Gorky's or Phillipe's, was a regular Philadelphia lawyer—talky, animated, brilliant even—but when he got back to the computer in his dismal room next door to a coin laundry in Koreatown, he'd clam up. *Just write the way you talk,* I'd tell him. Write the way you talk. That's what I kept trying to pound into his head, but it never did any good. Even fueled with amphetamines and espresso, it would take Cliff hours of ferocious grunting to squeeze out a few tiny rabbit pellets. Worse, he'd then seize upon a single precious pellet and polish it to a jewel-like brilliance. I often thought that Cliff English should have been a poet. Or a diamond cutter.

Cliff had published stories in *Stag* and other men's magazines when he was young, before turning to porn. He'd also written a detective novel that had been rejected by Vintage. He showed me the manuscript one day at Gorky's after our weekly story conference with Norma, and I have to say that it was well done. I lifted several phrases, in fact, because I liked the style. It was the Mike Hammer stuff. Short declarative sentences. Blunt, forceful. One. Two. Three. It was like writing with an adz.

There was a passage Cliff particularly admired in Joseph Conrad's novel, *Lord Jim*, about a storm coming up at sea. He's brought the book along with him, in fact, to Maria's.

"Listen to this, Donaldo. 'The gale had freshened since noon, stopping the traffic on the river, and now blew with the strength of a hurricane in fitful bursts that boomed like salvoes of great guns firing over the ocean.'"

Cliff closes the book and smacks his beer down on the table. "Man, I like that: *salvoes of great guns!* Conrad was lucky because he lived before TV fucked everything up for the printed word. We came along too late. Joseph Conrad got off a Polish merchant ship and jumped feet first right into the middle of literary England. He had *time,* you see. This is the 19th century we're talking about. Joseph Conrad

wrote *Heart of Darkness* with a fountain pen. He didn't need
Microsoft Word or a laptop computer. He didn't need *any*
of that shit. So you see, homes, this country—this
century—it's no place for us. We're displaced persons,
refugees. Know what? Really, you know what? I think I'm
gonna get my trick ass back over to Europe. That's the
place for guys like you and me. Or is it? Maybe we should
go to India. Or Bangkok. We could probably get a hearing
in Ireland. But we'd spend half our time dodging bullets.
Well, fuck Ireland! But, you know...I still believe in my heart,
Donaldo, that I'm going to crack it wide open. I've got a
book in me, I know it. I've got a book inside me and it's a
fucking blockbuster. My God, Donaldo, do you realize
what this is, what it could be? This could be...my *Paris
Book!*" He pronounces the words, "Paris Book" in a
hushed, reverent tone, misty-eyed, as if he were chanting a
litany over a holy relic. Then, patting my shoulder
reassuringly, "Don't worry, homes, I won't forget you. Shit,
man, we soldiered together. The streets of LA..."

It was always like that with Cliff when he got a few
beers. I don't mean the carping. I'm talking about the
hope. Cliff still thought he was going to get published. I'd
humor him, of course. I didn't want to spoil his dream. Far
be it from me to puncture a guy's balloon. Cliff thought
he'd be discovered. He really believed that in an editorial
office on Fifth Avenue his Maxwell Perkins was waiting
for him. He thought there are people in the world who
care about serious work.

The waitress brings two more Carta Blancas and our
bean burritos with sour cream. Cliff pushes his plate aside
and gulps down half of his beer.
"The day my Paris Book comes out, I'm gonna throw
some party, homes! The ballroom at the Westin
Bonaventure. Tits and champagne, brother! Ankhenaton
the Egyptian mummy man'll be there, and Queen Nefertiti
in her jiveass Rue de Faubourg Cinderella slippers. Those
motherfuckers will be taking dictation. *I'll* do the talking,

by Jesus, not some dried-up bundle of dead bones and mummy dust that's been rotting away in the fucking Cairo Museum since the fifth millennium before Christ! I'll go up on Mulholland Drive and I'll look out over the City of the Angels, and I'll be screaming, '*I am the great Louis-Ferdinand Céline and I piss on you all from a considerable height!*' Salvoes of great guns, baby! Salvoes of great guns!"

18

*I*t had been months since I'd seen Mickey Gilhooley, but one day in July he came to my door at Miraposa Street, a little drunker than usual, and a little sadder too, I thought. In fact he looked like he'd just crawled out of the San Andreas Fault. He insisted on buying me a corn dog and chili cheese fries at Der Wienerschnitzel and then we went to a bar. He said he'd been feeling low ever since he'd lost his job at Stanton's Market and his girlfriend had moved out, but after a few beers his eyes lit up as he confided that he'd been instant messaging with a Russian mail order bride he'd met on the Internet.

"Your Russian girls are solid, you know? They're...solid."

Doreen had gone to visit her ailing stepfather in Pacoima so I said what about meeting some real live Russian girls and Mickey said okay, so we went to the Las Palmas Ballroom on South Broadway where I was hoping to pick up where I'd left off with my old flame, Svetlana, but Svetlana wasn't available so I settled for a new girl named Natalya and Mickey met a beefy thug named Slovenka, who promptly stepped on his feet.

"Slovenka," Mickey muttered knowingly as we chugged a pint of Rittenhouse Monongahela Rye in the men's room between dances. "She's solid."

Slovenka was solid, all right. She could have squashed Mickey Gilhooley between her two fingers, but they hit it off like Mutt and Jeff and suddenly Mickey was once again the old Mickey Gilhooley, the Mickey Gilhooley I remembered.

"Where do you work a-John,
on the Delaware Lacawann,
a-wann, a-wann, a-wann!"

Mickey was sloshed to the gills. For weeks he'd been reading Turgenev in hopes of impressing the Russian mail order cutie, and after another trip to the can for a few more belts of firewater, he climbed up on a table and began spouting stuff like:

"Good evening, Vassily Andreyovich! Antonina Boganovich is waiting for you in the parlor. Would you like some tea?" Then, turning to me: "You hear that, bro? *Would you like some tea?* That's a great line! *Would you like some tea?* This is a writer, people. Turgenev! Ivan Sergeyevich Turgenev!"

Of course we got bounced out of Las Palmas, but not before we'd made a date with the girls.

Morning. After a trip to Der Wienerschnitzel for breakfast of sorts, we start in on the wine. Mickey's feeling down again and he needs to get his alcohol content up if we're going to do at all well with the girls tonight.

A month ago, Mickey informs me, he "put the plug in the jug" and joined the 12-Step Program, but he quickly became disenchanted with the whole business.

"After everybody spiels off their shit we go outside for a smoke break and everybody's pounding coffee like crazy, trying to catch a fucking coffee buzz. All they're doing is exchanging one addiction for another. It's bullshit. You know how people will say to a recovering alcoholic, I liked you better when you were drinking? Well, that applies to me. I liked me better when I was drinking."

"But one good thing did come out of the program. You know, I've never been a Republican or a Democrat or a Socialist or a Communist, and I'm not a Catholic or a Baptist or a Methodist or an Episcopalian, and I've never been a Raiders fan or a Denver Broncos fan. Fact is, I've never been to a football game, I never joined a church and I've never voted—do you see where I'm going with this? You've probably never voted either, have you?"

"Fuck no!"

"Well, you ought to think about it, Donzo. I don't mean voting, I don't mean that, but I mean...you ought to think about becoming a Democrat or a Christian or something..."

I felt like laughing in his face, but he was dead serious and I didn't want to upset his applecart.

"The thing is, you need a label in this world if you're going to be one of the bunch. Not a label exactly, but...shit, what is the word I'm searching for? Affiliations! Yeah, that's it. You need affiliations. Listen to this: Joe Jones, PhD, liberal Christian Democrat, president of the Rotary Club. See how great that sounds? There's a practical aspect to it too. They need to know that shit when they write your obituary. But coming back to what I was saying...you know, I don't have a BA or an MA or a PhD and I'm not a Mason or a member of the Elks Club or the Moose Lodge or what have you. I've never been anything, anything at all except a complete nothing. But now, thanks to the 12-Step Program I've got a title, a label. I'm somebody, I'm something: *I'm an alcoholic.* It's official, and by God, it feels good! I want to shout it from the housetops, *I'm an alcoholic! I'm an alcoholic!* I feel like I belong now, I mean to the human race. I'm a real person, a regular guy, and it's beautiful. I'm *one* of the motherfuckers."

Thanks also to the 12-Step Program he's been reading

the Bible and he's surprised to discover that he finds it interesting, even fascinating. "The Old Testament, not the New," he explains. "There's a big difference, you know. In the Old Testament God is right here on earth. He's in the burning bush and he's walking the Plains of Moab, and Jacob wrestles with an angel, and all of that, but by the time we get to the New Testament, God's gone MIA, he's long gone, over the hill, beyond the mountains, really far, he's way up above the clouds in his own private heaven, somewhere in the stratosphere, maybe as far away as the moon, twenty-eight million miles. He's turned his back on our lot and what's worse, everybody down here on earth is just sort of blasé about the whole business. So for my money the New Testament is baby shit by comparison. Compared I mean to the Old Testament."

We're out of wine so we cross Lafayette park and amble down to the Big Five Market on Rampart across from the Korean donut shop where I used to go for coffee every morning when I lived at the Wilshire Royale Hotel...and one morning, I recall, a young Salvadoran kid was shot to death right outside the donut shop by some cholos in a low-rider with a Yugo M70, and the bullets shattered the plate glass window. I'd just come out with my coffee. The kid went down and suddenly I was covered in blood, his or mine, I didn't know. I'd never taken a bullet in my life, and I'm thinking, "Hey, its not so bad after all, didn't hurt a bit." I even thought that maybe I was already dead, but it turned out that what I had was dozens of little cuts from the shattered glass. I was just glad it wasn't the kid's blood because the kid was dead as a duck. Those cholos really chopped him up. I got out of there before the cops arrived and I watched from my window at the Wilshire Royale when the meat wagon came and carted the body away. And a year later I was still picking glass fragments out of my left forearm...

Back at the park we plunk down on a bench with our wine. Reading the Bible got Mickey started on the Eastern religions and he's been reading some of the *Bhagavad Gita.*

"If you take a look at the Hindu Cosmology, they've got the whole business figured out, in terms of quadrants or whatever. The quadrant we're in right now, for example, is called the Kali Yuga. You probably know that. What it is, the Kali Yuga, is a kind of cosmic menopause. The Kali Yuga is called the Age of Darkness. We're right in the middle of one of the worst periods in human history. But the Kali Yuga, so they say, will be followed by the Satya Yuga, a Golden Age. Familiar story, isn't it?"

Back at Miraposa Street he gets going again on the Old Testament versus the New Testament. "Don't get me wrong. I'm not saying I like everything about the Old Testament. The whole thing about sex, for example, when Adam and Eve pick up on the fact that they're naked and cover themselves up with fig leaves. I mean, there's something a little bit sick about that, if you ask me. And the circumcision business, Genesis 17... It's as if the cock you're born with is somehow unacceptable. It has to be altered, trimmed like a vegetable, beautified, tricked up. It's almost like saying that God makes junk. The Bible tells us that we're made in the image of God, but apparently that's not good enough for us.

"Now we come to the thing about masturbation. Onan peeked into Tamar's tent and spilled his seed on the ground and this was wrong in the sight of the Lord and the Lord slew Onan. I don't know if that's an exact quote, but it's pretty close. But then you read in the Book of Numbers and Joshua and Judges that city after city falls to the Israelites—Moab, Bashan, Jericho, Gibeon, Beth-el—and time after time they kill everybody in the city—men, women and children. Read it for yourself. It's right there in the Bible. So it's perfectly okay to put an entire city to the sword, that's just fine in the sight of the Lord, but fool around with your weenie and the Lord is wroth. That's *streng verboten*, you see. Basically, what you get from reading the Old Testament is that sex is dirty and war is clean.

"What's more, even in the Bible you'll find discrimination against the unwanted man. Guys like me, I mean. It's right there is the Book of Genesis. For example, I can't get on the Ark. The Ark is for couples only. 'There went in two and two into the Ark, the male and the female, as God had commanded Noah.' *As God commanded!* The stallion and the mare, the boar and the sow, the stag and the ewe, the fox and the vixen, the lemur and the lemuress.

"See what I'm saying, Donzo? *Couples only!* I can't go to the new world. I can't get on the ship, I can't cross over the Jordan. I can't go to the Promised Land, because it's couples only! That's the rule! Is that discrimination or what? You remember where it tells how all the animals got on the Ark? 'Clean beasts and beasts that are not clean and fowls and everything that creepeth upon the earth.' You see? God didn't discriminate between clean beasts and unclean beasts. He didn't draw a line there. Your unclean beasts were allowed on the Ark—as long as they were paired up. There's your Couples Rule again. You could be the uncleanest son of a bitch that ever came down the pike, you could stink like a shithouse and you could still get on the Ark, as long as there were two of you and one of you was a girl. But show up without a date and you were fucking dead in the water. And I mean literally dead in the water, because it was right after this that the 'windows of Heaven' opened and the whole place was flooded. For forty days and forty nights! Well, you know the story.

"But what would things 'that creepeth upon the earth' be, do you suppose? I'm guessing it means things like salamanders and mud puppies, and beetles and centipedes and cockroaches. That's about as *creepeth* as you can get. But wouldn't that burn your ass, though? What it means is that a goddamn cockroach and his wife can get on the Ark but I can't!"

That night we all went out drinking at the Bitter End in Hollywood, and Slovenka got us started on the boilermakers.

"This'll put some fight in your pecker," she proclaimed as the four of us clinked glasses.

Slovenka was getting big ideas now that we were looped on boilermakers. She wanted to quit her taxi-dance job at Las Palmas and become a mud wrestler at Korky's Kingdom, a sinister biker bar in Encino. That's what she called thinking outside of the box. Mickey was ordering double shots of Goldwasser in between rounds of boilermakers and raving about Turgenev, and Natalya wanted to adopt a litter of feral kittens.

Natalya and I tried to dance to "Since I Met You Baby," but we ended up falling on the floor. Mickey, at the bar, was jawing endlessly with Slovenka. He was trying to talk her out of it, the mud wrestling, but Slovenka's sights were set on becoming one of Korky's Mud Angels. It wasn't going to be easy, she admitted. She'd have to work on her body slams and get her fighting weight down to 180. But Slovenka had stars in her eyes and the tryouts were coming up in just three weeks and there was no holding her back.

The two of them were drinking sidecars now, doubles, and I suddenly realized what a truly heroic drinker Mickey Gilhooley was. I couldn't begin to keep up with him. None of us could.

Then we went out on a boat—it may have been the next day—and I vomited over the rail at sunset into a rocking red-and-orange daubed sea. We were hitting the rye, the rye and the beer, but especially the rye, the Rittenhouse Rye. It was goofy. I never even liked the stuff.

I remember being in a room somewhere, maybe Laurel Canyon. An old woman with a single weeping eye told fortunes and her little dog's name was Edgar. We were trying to mellow out on tokay, but the sweet wine made Natalya upchuck so we went with a nice half gallon bottle of Absolut Vodka instead.

The Absolut Vodka got us to arguing, the three of us

versus Slovenka. We were dead set against the Korky's Mud Angel bit because none of us wanted to see Slovenka leave Las Palmas.

We wound up in Venice Beach, always a treat for me because of the nostalgic Coney Island ambiance. Close your eyes and you can feel the boardwalk under your bare feet, smell the cotton candy and watch the sobbing carrousel horses dance to the sad calliope music. We laced our morning coffee with Jack Daniels, then started pounding 40-ounce King Cobras. As our taxi pulled out of Venice Beach I saw the organ grinder sitting on a curb in the rain, with only a few nickels and pennies drowning in his mournful monkey's little tin cup.

"I forgot to tell you about the timetable," Mickey said, "back when we were talking about the Kali Yuga."

"Timetable?"

"Yeah, timetable. They've got it all figured out, the yogis and swamis and what have you. How long and all that. From the Age of Darkness where we are now until the dawning of the Golden Age..."

"Okay..."

"According to their calculations we'll enter the Satya Yuga, the Golden Age, right around 426,880 years from now."

Later that same day Mickey fell off the Santa Monica Pier. Hours after we'd pretty much given him up for lost he came lurching out of the ocean and staggered up to where we were sprawled on the sand under the pier drinking Gallo Zinfandel. My stomach was growling. I realized that I'd forgotten to eat, maybe for days.

Slovenka stood up and flexed her lats. "There's something about a kiddie pool filled with nice goopy mud that makes me just want to get in there and *wrestle*," she muttered fiercely.

"She'll be one of Korky's Mud Angels for sure," Natalya chirped confidently. "You better believe that shit, my friend. Keep your eye on this chick. She's going places.

A month from now we'll be watching her on YouTube."

Natalya had completely changed camps on us. She was totally buying into the dream, Slovenka's dream, the Korky's Mud Angel dream. She was even talking about becoming Slovenka's manager.

Suddenly it was night again, then morning, blinding bright, on the beach. The screeching gulls, the sandpipers, the everlasting surf. No sign of the Russian girls. Their troika had pulled out.

Mickey Gilhooley stood up, stretched, and fished a flat bottle of Rittenhouse Monongahela Rye out of his boot.

"Natalya's nice, but *Slovenka*. She's... She's solid. You know?"

"Yeah, I know."

The tide was coming in and the Goodyear Blimp was floating high above our heads. We emptied our pockets and spread our bills and change out on the sand. It came to $5.47, just enough it turned out for a hearty breakfast of corn dogs and chili cheese fries at Der Wienerschnitzel.

19

Donald O'Donovan, someday you're going to have to start being responsible for the magic that surrounds you."

That's what Norma Jacoby used to say to me during my Bareback Book days. That was another of her pronouncements along with "Los Angeles is the theater of our destiny." But it's true. Magic does surround me. It was July and I'd been pounding the pavement, looking for a job. A week before that I'd simply walked off a sign spinner gig. It was hotter than hell inside that bumblebee suit out there on Hollywood Boulevard. A bedraggled-looking kid came along. He was strung out and down on his luck. I stepped out of the bumblebee suit and the kid stepped in. We figured the boss would never notice. I had another job for three days as a waiter at a pizza joint, and I quit that one too. I had to wear a pirate costume and the guy never paid me.

It was a grim period, to say the least. Doreen, fed up with my bumbling efforts to land a job that would facilitate our new roles as Mr. and Mrs. Front Porch, kept going off in a huff to visit the relatives in Pacoima. She'd return from time to time to our love nest on Mariposa Street, but

things just weren't the same. I had a sneaking hunch that Mr. G was back in the picture, but my morale was now at such a low ebb that to be perfectly honest I didn't really care. And then one fateful day in August my relationship with the Oomph Girl came to an abrupt end. But more about that later.

And now for the magic. I was going into a tailspin, sinking lower and lower. I couldn't pay the rent. It was Grobbel's face that I saw now in the bathroom mirror. I didn't know what to do. Then, just when it seemed that everything had turned to shit, just when I was ready to throw up my hands and let fate have its way with me, I got a call from Oskie Oldham. He said he wanted to buy the film rights to *Nancy's Night with Noriega*. I didn't believe him at first. I thought he was joking. I mean, how do you make a horror flick out of a crotch novel? But Oskie was serious. *Nancy's Night with Noriega* would be a sequel to *Spurned, Slashed and Burned,* and a star vehicle for his nubile protégée Tatania Ferrari. His producer had found a guy in Pacific Palisades with the bling and they were ready to cut me a check for the rights.

Two days later we signed the papers sitting at an al fresco table at the International Restaurant, a homey little place on Hollywood Boulevard across the street from the Wax Museum.

It was beautiful the way it all fell together, a magical web of circumstance and seeming coincidence. If Fausto hadn't gone on that particular Tuesday night to the Spearmint Rhino strip club on Olympic, he wouldn't have run into our fellow Bareback Books author Colonel Wally Feathering ill from Cardiff-by-the-Sea, and if he hadn't mentioned to the Colonel that I was living at the Goat Farm in Reseda, the Colonel wouldn't have passed the news of my whereabouts on to Norma Jacoby and Norma Jacoby wouldn't have visited me on that magic day at the Goat Farm when she gave me back the film rights to *Nancy's Night with Noriega*—and if that fourth printing of

Nancy's Night with Noriega hadn't rolled off the presses precisely when it did Fausto wouldn't have passed the book along to Oskie Oldham and I'd still be gasping my lungs out in that bumfucked bumblebee rig on Hollywood Boulevard.

Here's what Oskie Oldham said to me that day at the place across from the Wax Museum: "Tatanya Ferrari is the real thing, man. She's got her boogie down. The camera loves her! She's got the star quality, that mysterious x-factor that nobody can quite put their finger on. You've seen her work. Tell me I'm wrong. We're looking at a young Sharon Stone here, an Angelina Jolie. And believe this: Tatanya Ferrari is *the* definitive Nancy. We had a little read-through the other day and Donald, she fucking *inhabits* the role."

I almost burst out laughing. Ferrari was a balloon-head and her acting was on a par with Fausto's. Oskie Oldham was the one who inhabited his role. Always the Director with a capital D, a regular Fellini. He declared over and over again that he was crazy about Tatania, and he was sincere, I never doubted that. Oskie Oldham was sincere about everything. Those close-set black eyes of his unfailingly burned with a feverish intensity. The man positively reeked sincerity. He told me later when we were both a little drunk how he knew that one day Tatanya would leave him for a younger man, her costar most likely, and how he'd already accepted that, and how it was footage he'd already shot in his head, and how he was okay, really okay, with it. He leaned across the table, cupping his chin in his hand—he had tears in his eyes— and told me in a voice hoarse with emotion how he knew in his heart that one day he'd open the door of her cage and she'd fly away from him, and he'd be really noble about it too, he assured me of that, and all the while you could tell that he was visualizing it as a film even as the words came out of his mouth.

We were pouring the beers down. It was a beautiful

summer afternoon and a loudly-perfumed whore strutted by, showing a mouthful of gold teeth. Oskie's words seemed to be coming to me now from a distant world. I had the check in my pocket, my ticket to a new life, and it was all running off beautifully, I mean in my mind. I was thinking of the little hotel near the Ponte Vecchio in Florence where Marlena and I once stayed, and the tiny trattoria with al fresco tables, the violins and the *ribollita* and the *frizzante*, and the waiters who obeyed us like dolls, and after the meal, espresso and a choice of gelatos. Our choice? *Spumone,* of course. *Spumone,* that's the word that was going through my mind, *spumone...*

Cliff English's suicide came as a shock. Was it the gray anonymity of Gotham or its spectacular promise that lured Cliff English back to New York to die? Or was it the desire to hurl himself kamikaze-like against the monolithic publishers' walls he couldn't batter down with words? We wondered, Fausto and I, did he plan it, rehearsing every detail in his mind as he rode all those weary miles on a one-way Greyhound bus ticket to take that beautiful final swan dive off the Brooklyn Bridge? Or was it a spur of the moment sort of thing? I suppose we'll never know for sure. The cops who fished Cliff's body out of the East River said he was doing 75 when he hit the water. Fractured skull, broken back, massive internal injuries. DOA, Calvary Hospital.

It was grim news, but a postcard the next day from Starz put me in a better mood. This time it was Belize. He was living in a VW bus at Caye Caulker with a girl named Samantha, and "Life here," he wrote in huge looping letters, "has a Reggae beat."

Right after my big payday I checked into the elegant Malibu Beach Inn, a room with a balcony overlooking the Pacific Ocean. The hotel wasn't far from the beach house

Starz and I once occupied. My room, I discovered, was stocked with boutique wines. I chose a 1999 Château Margaux because it resembled, at least in color, the cheap red wine we used to drink in Paris.

Stepping out onto my balcony with my wine at sunset was like stepping into the aftermath of a cosmic war. The brave sun, vanquished but spitting fierce yellow sparks, lay squashed on the horizon and the glowing red sky had become a harbor for incinerated clouds. "Château Margaux, the perfect Bordeaux, exploding with spice, earth and truffle scents," a carefully modulated voice seemed to murmur. I was drinking it straight from the bottle. Starz, good old Starz, Starz had bounced back, and I was thankful for that. Everything was coming up roses, not only for me and for Starz, but for everyone. Byron Lovelace was getting married, I'd learned. To a woman. This bit of intel from Sol Fingerbein, who'd recently landed a lucrative gig illustrating a Yiddish version of the *Kama Sutra*. Mickey Gilhooley was working as men's room attendant at the Pussycat Lounge, and Slovenka had a bun in the oven. Skylar? Skye was doing his thing at Dzuana's Open Mic in Amsterdam. And Cliff English...well... Here's to Cliff English. *Salvoes of great guns, baby!* You were right, Cliff, to write your Paris book in LA. Los Angeles is the cradle of the artist, not Paris. Paris is the past and New York is the past and Los Angeles, the world's most dynamic and demonic city, is the theater of our destiny.

The sun plunged at last into the fathomless black water, sputtering but defiant: *I'll be back, you bastards. You haven't seen the last of me yet!*

Another bottle of the Château Margaux. It was beautiful, beautiful, the way it had all gone down. For me it was the end of my personal Kali Yuga and the beginning of a new Golden Age. I was clear of the clockwork. No dollar options and no shaky back end deals. And no rewrites. Fausto will be doing the screenplay, Oskie informed me. He's also reading for the part of Noriega, and I'm betting he'll be a shoo-in. He's still got that old Fernando de León floy-floy.

20

I've been here in Tuscany for three months and I haven't written a word." That's what I told Fausto this morning on the phone.

Before leaving LA I noticed that the 1937 film version of *The Prisoner of Zenda*, starring Ronald Coleman as Rudolph Rassendlyll and Madeleine Carrol as Princess Flavia, was playing at the New Beverly Cinema. I didn't see the film, but on an impulse I got the book out of the library and the opening line reads like a leitmotif of my new life in Tuscany:

"I wonder when in the world you're going to do anything, Rudolph?"

Here in Tuscany I have everything a writer could want. A spacious room in a 300 year-old villa on a hill overlooking the 13th century village of Montefollononico. Wonderful Tuscan meals, incomparable French and Italian wines. I live like a count. A lightning-fast laptop computer, Microsoft Word, the Internet. All this and the companionship of my long lost half-sister, Solange. And yet I haven't written a line.

Yesterday I read three pages of *Papillon* in French.

Solange cleaned her brushes. We drank Chianti and *Vino Nobile di Montepulciano* and made black-olive *bruschetta* with our Italian friends in the villa's old world kitchen.

Later I did a few watercolors while Solange presided over me, waving her wooden spoon. I read some of Van Gogh's letters, in English. Writing to Theo from the lunatic asylum at Saint-Rémy, Van Gogh says, "*I am working with the enthusiasm of a man from Marseilles eating bouillabaisse.*" Now why can't I do the same?

I wonder when you're going to do anything, Rudolph?

Later. Maybe later, *domani,* tomorrow. And today? Today let's visit Florence, Siena, San Gimignano.

Beautiful Tuscany. You wake up in the morning and you want to say, "*Grazie, grazie!*" And everywhere you go, a rousing chorus of *buon giornos* and *buona seras.* Why was life so complicated in America?

This afternoon I returned from my wanderings to find Solange crowded into the kitchen with our Italian friends, cooking. That's what you do in Tuscany. You cook with friends. And cook we did. *Fegato* with garlic and fragrant fresh sage, *trippa alla Fiorentina,* and my two favorites, wild boar with sour apples and *fagioli all'olio.* And more *Vino Nobile di Montepulciano*, of course. And more and more.

I've come to the conclusion here in Tuscany that ideal working conditions are certain death to a writer. Maybe what a writer needs is to be locked up somewhere, like Van Gogh at Saint-Rémy, or like the Prisoner of Zenda. After all, didn't Cervantes write *Don Quixote* in prison?

I've been looking back, too...the package from Tuscany that day in October, my father's mandolin. The magic again, the mysterious way it all fell together, a magical web of circumstance and seeming coincidence. If my mother hadn't broken my father's mandolin over her knee Solange wouldn't have rescued the mandolin from the trash and lovingly repaired it, and she wouldn't have taken the mandolin with her to the orphanage in Willow Grove and kept it all those years as a memento of the father who abandoned her, and if she hadn't finally mailed the mandolin to me, we wouldn't have written back and forth across the ocean the way we did and I wouldn't be here today in beautiful Tuscany.

I've been looking back on everything, I mean the 20th century and my old life—my life on Sonrisa Street, the Labyrinth of Solitude and all that. Sonrisa Street was a wart in my karma. It was an enclosed arena where I struggled against invisible odds, a cell in which I squatted like a toad, bathed in my own cold sweat. Call it a psychotic episode if you like. Call it the tyranny of the mind. Maybe Sonrisa Street wasn't real. Or maybe only half-real. Maybe Sonrisa Street was a mirage. Or maybe "Sonrisa Street" is simply the name I've assigned to this particular period in my life. The crumbling old hotel? The Gypsy Lady? The somersaulting midgets? That little drowned rat of a dog? I'm not sure now. The whole episode has the ephemeral yet undeniable quality of a dream.

In any case, looking back, I understand perfectly what took place there, and why: *it was necessary to suffer in order to realize that the suffering was unnecessary.*

Doreen was real, certainly. But I was completely unprepared for what happened with Doreen. It came at me out of the blue. She'd returned from one of her trips to Pacoima in high spirits and everything seemed to be ducky for a change. We'd gone to the New Beverly Cinema, in fact, where they show the old movies, and we'd watched our all-time favorite flick, "It's a Wonderful Life," starring James Stewart and Donna Reed. Back at the apartment we sat on the couch with our bottle of Château de Puligny-Montrachet—just like old times—and we toasted: "To us!" And then Doreen said to me: "I'm sorry, Baby, but I can't sleep with you tonight."

"What are you talking about?" I said. I thought she was joking. But no, Doreen was deadly serious.

"It's Harvey. He's...he's asked me to marry him. And I said yes. I'm sorry, Baby..."

"Harvey..." I couldn't believe what I was hearing. I knew she was seeing other men, yes, sure, I mean, that was Doreen. I'd tried my best not to think about it. But *Harvey*...

"Baby, you're going to be famous someday. But you may be dead first. And I can't wait. Donald, listen...listen to me please. I'm thirty-seven years old. How much longer can I trade on my looks? You're a great writer. You know it and I know it. But right now you're balancing on shit..."

"Jesus Christ, Doreen. But...but...why Harvey?"

"Look, he's not the man you are. Our sex life won't be anything like what you and I have shared..."

"Then why—"

"Baby, I feel...I feel *comfortable* with Harvey. It's as if... Well, he does remind me of my father. I don't like the belching and I don't like the eyebrows and the dandruff and I don't like the cigars. But he's—he's—like...like...*family*. And," she added, carefully smoothing my hair, "he's buying me a Chevy Nova."

"Give me the fucking bottle," I said, and abruptly I burst into tears. It came out of me suddenly, like an orgasm—an orgasm of grief. I sobbed like an idiot for maybe three minutes, and then it was over. I guess I cared for Doreen a lot more than I wanted to admit, even to myself. Well, why not say it? Sure, I was in love with her, and it made me desperately sad to realize that our time together was over. But after my outburst I felt fresh as a daisy. *It's a Wonderful Life!*

I gave Doreen a chaste peck on the cheek. "I wish you every happiness," I said. "You deserve it."

"I never wanted to hurt you," she whispered, her eyes suddenly moistening. She threw her arms around me and held me tight for a moment, then she pulled away and gazed at me steadfastly.

"I told Klaus," she said, "and I told Ziggy. And Lars and Gustaf Metzger. Remember the twins from Duluth? And then I told Jaime—and Yves, of course—and Lefty and

Shloime and Rick—and Vincenzo. Dear, rumpled, right-off-the-boat Vincenzo! And that left you. Oh, Baby... I'm so sorry. I left you till last because I knew you'd take it the hardest. Can you ever forgive me? Believe me, Baby, telling you about Harvey and me is the hardest thing I've ever done because...because you're so damn *sensitive*." .